JUNKIE LOVE

JUNKIE LOVE

Joe Clifford

Battered Suitcase Press

JUNKIE LOVE

© 2013 by Joe Clifford

ISBN-13: 978-0615782959
ISBN-10: 0615782957

Battered Suitcase Press

An imprint of Vagabondage Press LLC
PO Box 3563
Apollo Beach, Florida 33572
http://www.vagabondagepress.com

First edition printed in the United States of America and the United Kingdom,

April 2013

10 9 8 7 6 5 4 3 2

Front cover art by Konstantin Kirillov. Cover designed by Maggie Ward.

NOTE FROM THE AUTHOR

Seems like I spent most my life working on this book: the first half screwing everything up and the next half writing it all down.

I began drafting *Junkie Love* about a month after checking into a long-term residential treatment program in Connecticut in early 2002. Actually, I began scripting my recovery memoir while I was still using. Toward the end of my run, I'd been crashing on my ex-wife's couch in L.A., in between stays in the Spring Street Shelter and psych ward, living off the wild orange trees that lined the boulevard. I'd dick around on her computer after she left for work. What I wrote was obviously a mess: incomprehensible, sprawling, didactic ranting, sprinkled with liberal misuse of semi-colons. Only one line from that original version remains, the very first I wrote, in fact (*All the ordinary people with their ordinary concerns...*). But I knew the experience was worth telling.

After I got clean, I returned to school, earned my degrees, and learned craft, all the while reworking raw material into something more cohesive (early incarnations began as a sci-fi/time-travelling odyssey with overt anti-religious and political overtones, and included a subplot involving very tiny monkeys—completely unreadable). Mostly, I sought to draw out the narrative, the actual *story*, the compelling part people appeared invested in. Despite the drugs and squalor, the book is really about a boy searching for a place he belongs.

Over the years, I've published several excerpts in literary magazines, journals, e-zines and quarterlies, giving readings in bookstores, at festivals and fairs, on NPR. People seem to like it. But the question is always the same: Is this story true?

And the answer is…I don't know.

That's not a total copout. Police and prosecutors will tell you, when it comes to trying criminal cases, eyewitness testimony is extremely unreliable and hard to hang a conviction on. You can't trust your memory of what you had for breakfast this morning, let alone a felony you may have witnessed. My friend Rich and I grew up together in Connecticut, diehard baseball fans. He likes the Red Sox; I bleed Yankee pinstripe. We both vividly recall the summer of 1983 when Dave Righetti no-hit Boston. It was the Fourth of July. Bright, sunny New England day. We were hanging out, swimming. Only he remembers hearing bad news in my backyard pool; I remember rejoicing at his cousin's cottage, thirty miles away. We can't both be right.

Junkie Love covers the ten or so years I spent on the skid row streets of San Francisco and traversing the lost highways of America. The overall arc of crimes, arrests, drugs and dirty sex is fairly accurate, as are the prevailing themes of fall and redemption. But is it true? That's tougher to answer. And not in any Philosophy 101/what is truth? sense. I mean, I *think* I'm telling the truth.

Except of course when I'm not. For the sake of storytelling, I combine trips, conflate characters, make up names, rearrange the order of events to streamline action and elicit the greatest emotional response. When enough details get changed, non-fiction can no longer ethically be called that, and once it's fiction, you're working with a new set of specs. Or in the words of my dear writer friend Andrea Askowitz: Never let the facts get in the way of a good story.

I can tell you this. When I do outright lie, it tends to be about the little things, like there was a different song playing was on the radio when she broke my heart, or the car I stole was actually a truck. The major events and really disturbing scenes? The ones that make you gasp and shudder and feel like you need to take a shower, where you say to yourself, as you scrub and scratch at the dirt that won't come off, "No *way* that is true…" 99.9 percent of the time, happened just the way I say it did.

Of course, one of the problems with the junkie memoir is it's hard to trust the narrator. I am better now. But drug addicts are notorious liars, and your mental faculties are, at best, skewed.

I remember copping one San Francisco afternoon with my buddy, Tom Pitts, and pointing out a cute kid standing across the street in a karate outfit.

"Hey," I said. "Look! A little black belt."

Tom panned over, squinting, then back to me, puzzled. "Dude," he said, "that's a fire hydrant."

False memories. Misinterpretation. Shifting points of view and suspect agendas. Ulterior motives. Blunt head trauma, poor nutrition, and poly substance abuse. So much shit gets in the way of trying to tell the truth, sometimes it's easier if you don't bother classifying it and just move on.

So here it is. My novel. My memoir. Fact or Fiction. Whatever you label it, it will always be the story of my life.

In loving memory of my mom

JUNKIE LOVE

PART ONE

Sugar and Bleach

1.
Hepatitis Heights

We call this place Hepatitis Heights. It's a shooting gallery on top of 23rd Street, Potrero Hill, San Francisco. I guess you could say I live here. It's where I shoot my dope and crash when I'm not in somebody's trailer under the freeway or at the music studio off 3rd Street. The Heights is where I keep the few things I still own: an extra T-shirt, toothbrush, some cartoons I've drawn. But I don't pay rent. Nobody does. It's been almost a decade since I left my small hometown in Connecticut to follow the lead of my heroes: Kerouac, Burroughs, Westerberg, the call of the rock 'n' roll drifter. That was 1991. I was twenty-one. Now I am stuck here. It's 1:30 p.m. and I've switched on the TV show *Cops*. I have a tiny black and white television they will not take at the pawn shop, despite my numerous pleas.

Hepatitis Heights is a flat with three bedrooms and a bathroom on the right, boxed in by a spacious kitchen and quaint breakfast nook at the end. The fading pastel exterior resembles many of the Victorians you find in San Francisco. Except this place is filled with junkies and speed freaks. We don't allow crackheads here. Even among drug addicts, there is a hierarchy.

When Catherine, my wife, and I first moved in, we got dibs on the front room, the one with the big bay windows overlooking the winding hills of San Francisco and its shimmering bay. Cathy has schizophrenia. We painted the room hospital green to remind her of home, and for a while, it really was home.

But she's gone now.

These days, people trade goods and services to sleep in the bathtub. There is no telephone or running water. We have no electricity. An extension cord hangs out my window, hooked up to the basement apartment of the guy living downstairs, an old transvestite named Henry, who lets me use his. Months-old trash is piled up in our hallway, because the city will not pick up your garbage if you don't pay your bill. All through the night, tweakers crawl around inside the walls, rummaging through the busted vacuum cleaner parts and gasoline-soaked rags, inside cubbyholes and storage spaces, searching for anything to sell.

I'm still in the front room I once shared with my wife, the bay windows now lacquered black. Long velvet drapes snatched from the thrift store on Valencia and 16th, slightly stained with grease and cum, give the room its majestic, low-budget-adult-film feel. I'm not sure of the players in the company today. We have a rotating cast. At any given time, there can be more than twenty desperate, addicted criminals in this place. I lock my door at night. But that doesn't stop the mice from crawling through my hair.

I am mostly a heroin addict at this point, having graduated from strictly meth a while ago, moving through the ranks, like snorting to the needle. But I will shoot up anything, coke, speed, fentanyl fished from the dumpsters behind SF General, whatever you put on the table. I like to believe I'm still more lucid than the average tweaker. Call me the One-eyed King.

I've found a vein in my big toe for my wake-up fix. I blew out the big veins. All I have left are the tiny ones in my fingers and toes, and, of course, I have my cock. But they warn you about shooting up there at the needle exchange, where graphic pictures of black, necrotic tissue scare me off.

I've mined a few cigarette butts from empty beer bottles in the trash and am drying them out in the dirty, white microwave I keep in my room. Waiting for the bell to ring, I see on TV that the cops have raided a meth lab in the garage of a house belonging to an old woman. Her adult son, apparently the cook, is being interviewed. His jaw slings low and responds unnaturally when he tries to talk, as if it's unattached from the rest of his face. This is a common speed freak phenomenon, the result of constant teeth grinding, a precursor to meth mouth, which is what happens when the drug's acidity corrodes the gums and rots the teeth to little, brown nubs.

As I watch the man on TV struggle to speak, a piercing scream echoes throughout Hepatitis Heights, followed immediately by the jarring sounds of kicked-in doors and shattered glass. Then come the sirens and stomping boots, the bullhorns and shouts of "Police!" German Shepherds bound up the steps, barking angrily.

An M-16 aimed at my head, I am ordered out in the hall and against the wall. The cops rouse the two smelly girls who each paid me a dollar to sleep on my floor and tell them to do the same. Sunlight streams through the open front door, bright yellow beams clogged with the dead cells of the dying, causing the other vampires to shield their eyes and hiss.

The drugs I shot up navigate my bloodstream, filtering through my liver and striking pay dirt in the receptors of my brain, optic nerves tingling in a morphine dream.

United States Federal Agents and the San Francisco Police are everywhere. They're swarming the place, breaking down doors, popping up through cracks in the floorboards, sliding down shingles and swinging through widows. And this will only piss off our neighbors more; they've been trying to get us evicted for months.

Out the front door, a dozen squad cars and a big, black S.W.A.T. van are jacked up on the curb, officers crouched behind, two-fisting their firearms, which are pointed squarely at us.

Inside, police drag tweakers from rooms and closets, out from under tables and into the hall; they don't put up much of a fight. They seem paralyzed, faces frozen, locked in the grimace of a nightmare. This is the day they pray isn't real. Methamphetamine produces intense paranoia, so addicts must convince themselves on a daily basis that the government is not stalking them with video cameras, that no one is taping their phone calls and there are no monsters living under their bed. So you can imagine how difficult this moment is for them, this melding of fear and reality.

The officers keep shouting, "Get down!" or "Get up!" or "Up against the wall—now, asshole!" and I can't tell whether it's coming from the TV or the ATF or if it's all in my head.

I am having a tough time keeping my left arm up. I got out of SF General yesterday. I fell off my bike and broke my collarbone on my way to score, and my arm is in a sling. As soon as I got back to Hepatitis Heights, a guy I'd ripped off for twenty bucks came by and picked a fight with me, and the collarbone separated again.

The door to my room is open, and I see tourniquets, used needles, little balls of cotton, the bite-size packets of antibiotics they hand out at the needle exchange scattered about the floor. One of the cops sees this, too.

He asks if he can search for contraband.

I ask, "Can I say no?"

He says, "Yes, you can say no."

So I say, "No."

See, they are not after me today. Nor most of my other roommates. They are after this one tweaker who lives in the back, an ex-con named Donnie who has warrants out. Most of us have warrants out. But ours are for little things, like stealing paint from Home Depot or buying needles from an undercover cop in the park. Donnie's crime involved guns and shooting at police.

I look down the hall and see some of the new tenants for the first time—dirty, scary, whacked out of their skulls. Everybody stinks. Nobody has shoes.

And this is my life. I am thirty years old. I don't know where my wife is. I have lesions peppering my face. My arms are riddled with abscesses. I am six feet and one inch tall, and I weigh one hundred and fifty pounds. When I first became addicted to drugs shortly after arriving in San Francisco, I told myself I was just a white, suburban kid playing the part of a scumbag junkie. It will give me material for an album or book I'll write someday; I am not like these other people. But today, as the ATF drags Donnie away to San Bruno Prison over the din of television theater, and as the rest of the Heights' death-sentence kids drag themselves into their respective dark corners to inhale aluminum foil or cook up a fix or just beg for a twice-pounded cotton, I realize I am not playing a part anymore; I really am a scumbag junkie. And I don't know how I am going to get home.

2.
Candy and Cigarettes

A few months after the Hepatitis Heights raid, in the summer of 2000, after I get sick of the endless scamming for a fix, the fruitless searches for a vein and daily humiliation of eating food that other people throw away, I phone my mother in Connecticut and tell her I am ready to straighten out my life. Again. It takes some wrangling, but she buys me a plane ticket back home. This has been my routine for the last couple years. Every few months, I make the call, and my mother, desperate to believe in her son again, always falls for it.

I will check into rehab; I have to recharge my battery. You can only stay out there so long before a break is necessary and you need to get your habit in check, roll back the tolerance clock. The lifestyle wears you down. Money's been harder to come by lately, as more friends are getting arrested or dying or just disappearing into the night, and my measures to stay alive have grown increasingly desperate, bringing me one step closer to my greatest fear: prison.

Rehabs are better on the East Coast; I never check into the San Francisco ones. They're too hardcore, run by the jacked-up convicts and behavioral modificationists of Walden House and Delancy Street. It'll be good to see my mother. She's pretty sick.

I bring enough dope with me so that I won't go into withdrawal. They will give me methadone once I'm in treatment, so I shouldn't suffer much of a kick.

I stay with my mom at her condo for a couple days and try to smile encouragingly when she talks about her faith and how this will be the time I finally turn it around. After she goes to work, I lounge on the big couch, flipping through hundreds of channels of cable television, shooting up heroin and eating her ice cream.

My mother drives me up from Connecticut to the Briarpatch Retreat in Vermont and helps me fill out the paperwork, waiting to leave until I am admitted. The Briarpatch Retreat is my favorite rehab.

Nestled in the Vermont countryside on sprawling acres of rolling meadows, it's like a country club, with tennis courts and softball fields, a weight room and an Olympic-sized swimming pool, with meals catered by the Marriott and private patient rooms. After months of batting away mice and ducking ex-cons looking to rip me off at Hepatitis Heights, it's a pretty sweet deal.

In rehab, I am a rock star.

It's a great place to meet girls. I'll get some numbers, call when I get out, we'll party, have a good time, before I'm on my way back to California.

It's not like there's a lot of competition on the ward. The guys in here are usually in bad shape, overweight, going bald, missing teeth. But there's never a shortage of attractive girls, and let's face it, you're catching them when their self-esteem isn't at an all-time high. Twenty-eight days on a locked ward; it's like shooting fish in a barrel.

A guy like me only needs two things to pick up girls on the inside: candy and cigarettes. Junkie girls going through withdrawal crave the sugar, and there isn't much to do in-between groups on proper nutrition, emotional triggers, and relapse prevention besides smoke. On our way in, I had my mom stop at 7-Eleven so I could stock up on both.

After a couple weeks of eating right, sleeping, and putting some pounds back on, I'm looking good. I have become very popular with the other patients. I am always the most popular guy in rehab. I tell the best stories; everyone laughs at my jokes. At night, I play the unit's guitar on the smoking porch. People gravitate to me. In high school, I hung with the ugly people in the art room. Back then, I was undersized and unremarkable, a creep and a weirdo. In here, I'm quarterbacking the goddamn team.

I notice her the moment she walks onto the floor.

Her name is Amy, and she's pretty. Really pretty. Winona Ryder pretty. On her first night in, while the rest of the unit attends an AA meeting, I stay behind to be alone with her on the smoking porch. She's shaky because they don't give you methadone until you see the doctor, and when she came in, the doctor had already left for the day.

I make small talk with her, do my charming, nervous guy thing. I can tell that she likes what I'm selling, but she's hurting. I say I have just what she needs. I light up a Camel and offer her some Skittles.

The next day, we're making eyes at one another over breakfast, exchanging notes like teenagers after group, playing telephone with other patients and passing messages down the line to see if we "like" each other. You're not allowed to have romantic relations in rehab, but soon, Amy and I are eating our meals together, holding hands in the patient lounge when no one's looking; then we're kissing around corners and under the stairwells, feeling each other up in the bathrooms.

I hadn't spoken to my wife, Cathy, in almost a year when she got a hold of me at my mother's house a few weeks back. We've been speaking regularly since. My wife is living in Los Angeles now, sober after having completed a long-term residential program in Hollywood. She sounds good, clearheaded and determined, like she's working "the program," which is what they call it in recovery when addicts are doing the right thing, attending AA meetings and taking personal moral inventories. Cathy says she wants me to come visit her when I am clean.

Even though we haven't lived together for a long time, I still love my wife. Very much. It's just that I love something more.

A week and a half after I meet Amy, we check out of rehab together.

For the next seven months, I am consumed. Amy and I head cross country to San Francisco, fucking through Nebraska cornfields while I drive, and she bunches her skirt, pulls her panties to the side and straddles me as tall stalks whisk by on a lost highway. We shack up in Tenderloin flophouses, get arrested, have our hotel rooms raided, get collared by the cops. Amy and I fuck and fight incessantly. We lie and steal money from banks and live a life on the run. And when our crimes finally catch up with us and we are forced apart, and she flees San Francisco for the safety of her parents' home in Vermont, I am right on her heels, because I cannot live without her. She is the best running partner I ever had.

People who aren't addicts will ask me later, after the crash, what it was I saw in Amy. They will not understand how I could've been so crazy about the girl. They will say she didn't seem particularly bright or like she cared about me, and that aside from the way she looked, she didn't have much going for her. And they will be right. But they don't understand junkie love. When you're as sick and addicted as we are, the rules to that game change. When you've just banged a speedball up your thigh and have finished going down on each other, and you lay collapsed, half naked, pants by your ankles, tourniquet still wrapped around, you can't tell if it's the orgasm or the rush of the narcotics that is making you feel so needed, so loved, so perfectly at peace with your disjointed world, because there is no division anymore, not from you, or from her, or from the drugs; it is one big tingling pleasure center, and it is viral and it is parasitic.

Amy will be my heroin.

It is wintertime and very cold in early February 2001. We are in a roadside motel in Rutland, Vermont, a miserable, little town.

I wrote a song for Amy. Its first line, stolen word-for-word from Tom Waits: "I'll love you, baby, 'til the money runs out." And the money has run out. We are out of scams. Out of lies. Out of hope. We have warrants out for our arrest. My mother is dying, and I desperately want her to see her oldest boy clean before she goes.

At thirty-one, I have taken this as far as it can go.

Slate skies hang low over one-lane roads packed with mud and sludge and snow, as one storm blends into the next.

We pay for the night with the last of our money, shoot up everything we've got and fuck our way through dawn until we are empty. Now it is morning. Check out time is 11 a.m. The sickness will be coming soon, and I know that despite our promises to stay together, I am losing her.

Amy fell asleep on her stomach. I sit naked on the floor and watch her, the New England light graying her skin, wishing I could stop time, find a way to place us both in a box for all eternity, because nothing good is going to be happening to either one of us for a very long time.

The clock reads 10:46. I know, because I am looking at it when they come.

When the police come for you, it is pretty much like in the movies. They bang loudly, but before you can answer, the door is kicked in, and you are spread eagle on the floor, hands cuffed behind your back, and ordered not to talk or they'll shoot.

They drag Amy and me outside and throw us into the backs of separate cruisers before I have a chance to ask her if she has any cigarettes left. Her car pulls away first. I know not to turn around. I know doing so will be a mistake. But I do it anyway.

As the taillights recede into the gusting Vermont snow, I catch that sad, lonesome wave goodbye from the rear window, and I know she is never coming back. And I am alone again, scared, looking up at a mountain I am too tired to climb.

When you say goodbye to someone at an airport or a bus station (or from the back of a police car), do not turn around. If you do, you'll regret it for the rest of your life.

3.
My Wife

The health inspector arrived early in the morning.

This would've been the winter of 1995, shortly before Cathy and I married. Or it could've been just after. She'd called the San Francisco Health Department, which was something she often did, phoning public officials whenever she was having a schizophrenic episode and feeling like unseen malevolent forces were attacking her. The Health Department. Social Security. PG&E.

We lived on 23rd Street in those days, too, but on Bryant, well below SF General Hospital and Hepatitis Heights, which didn't exist yet. Cathy had been at the window for hours, throwing crumpled notes at passersby. She'd scribbled instructions to "knock it off" or she'd "contact the proper authorities." Everything was a conspiracy to Cathy.

The three of us stood awkwardly in the kitchen. Cathy held an empty travel sewing kit, the kind you find at all-night gas stations next to the single-dose packets of aspirin. She'd been up all night using a butter knife to scrape the crud out of every orifice in the apartment—from the grout of floor tiles, under the stove broiler and tub feet, between the top shelves in the pantry. She said it was evidence of the killer molds and spores that had been planted to poison us and insisted they be passed along to the Center for Infectious Diseases in Atlanta, before prattling on about the CIA and, of course, the Freemasons.

Everything was a plot involving the Freemasons and the number 23. I'd learned about the number 23 from an old bass player. I never should've told her about that damn number, because once you notice it, it is everywhere. It didn't help that she was 23 years old, living on 23rd Street, and sleeping with the 23rd guy she'd ever had sex with.

Cathy had recently been released from a 5150, California's seventy-two-hour, court-ordered hold in a psychiatric hospital, after she'd walked into the ER saying she was possessed by an incubus. They'd put her on the Thorazine-Haladol-Zyprexia cocktail and sent her home. The cocktail wasn't helping, as she had become increasingly convinced I'd contracted the Ebola virus and would need to be quarantined. A few months earlier, one of my drug buddies, Ray, a jittery, little guy with giant glasses on a humongous head, had forgotten his book on microscopic household pests at our apartment, and I'd been fighting an uphill battle since. Cathy was extremely open to suggestion. If she saw a TV show about botflies, you could be certain later that night, she'd be clawing at every red dot on her body until she drew blood.

It was getting harder for me to take care of her, and I'd resorted to feeding her handfuls of Valium, trying to put her under for days at a time. But Cathy had learned to cheek the pills. Some mornings I'd awaken and if I hadn't secured her during the night, she'd be gone, and I'd get telephone calls from strange men telling me there was a young lady there who said I was dead.

The health inspector looked at me, puzzled. I shrugged.

Cathy was trembling, hand outstretched, offering her evidence. "What's wrong with you people? Why can't you see it?"

I met Cathy at Gluehead's shack the preceding summer. Gluehead was our speed dealer. But he was much more than that. We called ourselves the Gluehead Army. There were a lot of people in the Gluehead Army. There was Sanger, who was Glue's right hand man, and Brian Fast, at least in the beginning until he screwed everyone over. And then there was Pence and Big Tom and Leif Irish and Ray. There were others, too. I only did speed back then. That's all any of us did. We were all rock 'n' rollers.

Glue was a great storyteller. Because of all the speed he took, his short-term memory was kind of fucked. So whenever he told a story, he'd forget that he'd told it many times before. Each time he told a story, he did so very enthusiastically.

My favorite was The Prison Story.

In it, Gluehead is in San Bruno Prison. One day he gets out of the shower to discover a bunch of big and nasty brothers have taken all his cigarettes. Now, if that's me in the story, I don't do a goddamn thing; I let them have my cigarettes. But Glue said that if you do that sort of thing in prison, it makes you a little bitch, and if you're not sold for a deck of playing cards by the end of the night, you can at least count on never eating dessert again. What Glue does, he pops the razor blade out of his shaver, and he walks over to those brothers, who are standing there, smoking his cigarettes, and he slices his own hand down to the bone.

Gluehead holds up his bloody hand. He says, "Those are *my* cigarettes and I want them back. I'm real sick. You don't want my blood on you."

Gluehead gets his cigarettes back.

A piano prodigy-turned-skateboarding-punk-turned-speed-freak legend, Gluehead lived in a nineteen-by-eight foot shack in the Lower Haight on the back edge of some property belonging to his ex-girlfriend, who was a much bigger dealer. She dealt to the big boys; Gluehead dealt with people like us. Gluehead still played piano. He was really good at one time, I heard. He was really good when I knew him, too. But it was different because of the drugs.

There was electricity in the shack via a generator but no toilet or shower, no refrigerator, no stove. Tweakers don't sleep much, so Glue didn't need a bedroom, but he had a mattress anyway and a coffin that he sometimes crashed in. The place was overrun with crap. There were toppled shelving units and jagged light bulb bases and spent lighters, paint thinner, books, broken furniture piled high next to spread-out clusters of dismantled radios and tape decks, milk crates and mountains of unwashed, picked-from-the-street clothes. Instruments in various states of decay lay scattered throughout the place—half a guitar here, a keyboard missing keys there, a snare drum, a horn. There were giant cord balls everywhere, instrument cables that had become so intertwined they looked like snakes writhing in heat. The shack was basically a storage shed whose construction had been halted. It certainly wasn't up to code for human occupancy. You could see the exposed beams and two-by-fours, the anchors and joists and clipped electrical wiring, the mangy, pinkish-brown insulation, which was waterlogged and smelled like old tuna fish. It got very cold in the shack at night, and the roof leaked in the rain.

It was one of the best homes I ever knew.

A student at UC Berkeley who'd call Gluehead to score from time to time, Cathy came from upper crust in Regent, Minnesota. I can't say whether she had schizophrenia back then. I know she drank a lot. I think the signs of her sickness were there, had I known what I was looking for.

Cathy's cousin, Rhonda, had flown in from St. Paul, and the two of them had stopped by the shack looking for speed before hitting the downtown nightclubs. There wasn't any, though. Hadn't been for a while. The Feds had popped a major Mexican cartel a few weeks earlier, clogging the pipeline; the whole city was dry. We were all hurting.

You didn't see girls like Cathy at the shack often. Beautiful, yes, but there was something otherworldly about her, too. Long, straight, black hair with a face as white as porcelain, she reminded me of a doll. She wore a short, magenta dress that night and was so drunk at one point that when she tried sitting on Glue's lap, she fell over and her legs spread apart. As she lay on the floor laughing, I saw her panties. They were royal blue. It would be one of the few times I'd ever hear her laugh. I couldn't have known that then. The way she carried on, Cathy came across as vivacious, the life of the party, a girl most comfortable at the center of attention. Not even close. I'd later learn that, without the alcohol, Cathy was cripplingly shy and further withdrawn into herself than anyone I've ever met.

I had to work in the morning, but I let Cathy drag me out with her. The nightclub was awful, and my not being high made that thumping techno music excruciating. I've always hated crowds, everyone dancing and hopping like a fool. I didn't have the energy to be charming, and I just wanted to go to sleep. I had a loft where I was squatting—a nice loft, as far as squats go—and a job at the airport. I was one of the few guys who even had a job in those days. While most of the Gluehead Army just hung around the shack waiting for Glue to kick down free drugs, I was actually responsible, earning money to buy my drugs by delivering important documents from cargo planes. (I'd be fired two weeks later when they'd find speed in my delivery van.)

I was surprised when Cathy said she wanted to see me again. I don't think she could've known how hopeless I was. It wasn't until she was gone for the night that I started to fall in love with her.

Before our second date, I went to Kerrie's house. Kerrie was a stripper and older than I was. I'd once told her that life is over after thirty. I was twenty-five. She was thirty-four. I needed to shower and borrow some clothes. My squat didn't have a shower, and Kerrie always had nice men's clothes lying around. Her marriage to John Wayne Newton had dissolved by then, and we'd sometimes fuck. John Wayne was one of the Boys of Belvedere, the first friends I made in San Francisco, before the drugs made things like friendship expendable.

Kerrie was in love with me, and I was sort of in love with her. She was a knockout—a blonde-haired, big-titted, blue-eyed girly-girl, the sort that knocks *anyone* out. I'd once suggested while she was still married that we run away together to Arizona, leave this city behind. Even then, I could see where my life was headed if I stayed in San Francisco. I was half joking. When she said, "Let's go," she wasn't kidding. Kerrie scared the hell out of me.

After I showered and got dressed, I asked to borrow money so I could buy flowers for my date.

Cathy and I had made plans to meet at Glue's shack, but she never showed. I sat there, with my stupid hair combed and clean clothes ironed, holding those damned flowers, for hours.

Around 1:30 a.m., Gluehead said we should go to a bar. It was cold, the fog rolling in. San Francisco, where sometimes it got so dark and gloomy you felt like a ghost walking on the moors. I was depressed. If I liked Cathy before she stood me up, I was in love with her now. Glue put his arm around me.

"Why are you always so nice to me?" I asked him.

"I've always been a sucker for a sensitive boy," he said.

That was Glue, a sensitive thug. One minute he'd be fending off convicted murderers, like the time Earl Clutch, a maniac fresh out of San Quentin, was pounding on Gluehead's ex's door and Glue stared him down, and the next, he'd be saying something like that.

Coming over Buchanan Street, this little hill with a church at the top, a Buddhist temple, I think, the streets were dead, soundless, not even traffic coming off the 101, whose off-ramp was Fell Street, which became a straight shot to Golden Gate Park, which usually meant traffic, no matter what time of day or night.

From out of the shadows, this black kid on a bicycle came flying over the hill from the direction of the Webster Street projects a few blocks away. His front wheel slammed down, and he flipped over the bars, face scraping along the asphalt. Jumping to his feet, frantically reaching for his bike, one foot on the pedal, spinning a wild 360° in the oily mist, the kid hauled ass out of there. Right behind him came the police, two squad cars, lights whirling, sirens slicing through the murkiness, taking air like the *Streets of San Francisco*. They blew past us like we weren't even there.

Glue was staring at the spot where the kid crashed. "You see that?"

"Kid's going to jail. So?"

"No, that!" Glue said, pointing.

In the middle of the road lay fifty, maybe a hundred tiny baggies, each one packed with crack cocaine.

For the next few weeks, people stopped by the shack, hoping the meth drought was over. Glue broke the bad news. "But there's some crack," he said. The speed freaks sighed, hung their heads. In a corner, a pipe was all set up with Brillo pads and a blowtorch. Glue didn't ask for money. The speed freaks muttered how it was better than nothing, and then begrudgingly smoked some rock, spitting out fumes, angry at the government. They left ten minutes later. They didn't even say thank you. And Gluehead didn't expect them to.

It was funny. Just over that hill, there were people in those projects fighting, stabbing, shooting each other— people who'd sell their own mother out—for a crumb of the stuff, and here we were, a bunch of tweakers, acting like we'd been forced to suffer handjobs from the pretty girl's less attractive best friend.

■

I finally got that second date, after which Cathy asked me to move into her Berkeley apartment, which was good timing since the sheriffs were about to toss me out of my squat any day. Cathy's parents paid her rent and bills as long as she was in school, so we were free to spend more money on crystal meth.

Cathy was what we called a "weekend warrior," someone who dabbles in the lifestyle, getting high after work or class, snorting a line or two on the weekend. I was a full-time tweaker, and she tried to keep up with me, and she wasn't wired to do that.

Amphetamine psychosis is a fairly common side effect, but I didn't know that's what was happening at the time. Her sickness revealed itself slowly, like when she told me one day she'd overheard the hairdresser saying she had lice, which wasn't true and would've been a shitty thing to say, but people say shitty things that aren't true all the time. Or like when she said she saw our landlord hauling out a very large, black trash bag, and that the cops were downstairs asking questions. Kind of creepy, but plausible. The night terrors and seeing demons didn't start happening until after she dropped out of school, and we moved to the city and got that apartment on 23rd and Bryant.

If the seed of Cathy's sickness had already been planted, I was the shit in the fertilizer that made it grow. By then, I could see she wasn't well, and I spent a lot of nights on the phone fighting with her parents, who wanted her back home in Minnesota so they could lock her up and get her the help she needed. I viewed their influence as stifling. I wanted to control her fate, because I thought I was going to free her. I was young. I was headstrong. I was wrong.

We were married in Reno less than a year after we met.

Sanger agreed to be my Best Man. Leif Irish used to describe Sanger as an even more cantankerous Denis

Leary. Which is a pretty accurate description. They certainly looked alike, although Sanger's hair was a lot longer. Like Leif, Sanger played the drums. He'd been in a lot of bands over the years, F17, Rocket Racer. He was really good, although by the time I met him, nerve damage from the meth was affecting his timing. Like Glue, he was older than the rest of us, and we all looked up to him. But lack of sleep and living in a cramped storage unit in an alley behind 16th Street made Sanger mean as a cornered badger.

Junkie Jason was over at our apartment this one time. Junkie Jason was the guy who'd eventually turn me onto heroin. Sanger was there, too. We were all watching a movie, *The Rock*, I think, and Jason had just fixed some smack and wouldn't shut up. Sanger was strictly speed. He detested any kind of downer. Once, when Brian Fast admitted to smoking pot to alleviate back pain, Sanger barked, "Man, I bet you didn't even try Advil!" Junkie Jason was yappy all through the movie, the way junkies get after shooting up, opiates warming him friendly, making him loving as hell. Sanger finally turned around and said, "Shut up, you stupid junkie." He didn't scream it or anything, just said it as calm and cruel as the light of day. You could see the high instantly drain from Junkie Jason's face; he didn't say another word for the rest of the afternoon. I don't think he ever recovered.

When I called my mother and told her that I was getting married, she was very happy. She had no idea what I was turning into. My mother sent me her wedding ring. My parents had been divorced for a long time and they didn't speak. Although my father eventually became small-town rich—a four-bed, three-bathroom saltbox on two acres in the Connecticut suburbs—when they'd married, they were in their teens and poor, and the diamond was small, and he never cared enough to upgrade. My mother's giving it to me meant a lot. Someone would steal that ring before the wedding, though. It would take me a long time to find out who. But I'd find out. And I'd have my revenge.

After I proposed, Cathy's folks had managed to pry her back to Minnesota briefly, where they'd had her hospitalized. But I'd gotten her back. Ray, who'd left that book on household pests, gave me the $100 I needed to buy her a bus ticket. He put a blank envelope into the Bank of America depository and made a withdrawal against non-existent funds. Back then, banks trusted you when you said you'd put a check in the envelope. It was no small favor. Even though he was a drug addict, Ray took his credit seriously.

Cathy's cousin, Rhonda, flew in for the wedding. I didn't have a lot of time. One of Cathy's ex-boyfriends, this really old guy named Stan, who was like eighty, had been hired by her parents on a recon mission, sent to stop the wedding, get me out of the picture and bring her back home for good.

Cathy once told me a funny story about Stan, who used to work for the CIA. That's not the funny part. Even though Cathy was paranoid about that stuff, after having met Stan, I am pretty sure she was telling the truth with that one. She'd dated him before me. They met at Chez Panisse, Alice Waters' restaurant at the foot of the Berkeley Hills. Shortly into their relationship, Stan could see that Cathy wasn't well, and, concerned, he called her mother. Cathy did not like people talking to her mother behind her back; she considered it the ultimate betrayal. The next time Stan came over to her apartment, Cathy asked if he wanted to have kinky sex. Of course, he did! She had him lie naked on the bed and tied him up. Then she walked to her closet, grabbed a plank of wood, and beat the shit out of him, all the time screaming, "Don't talk to my mother! Don't talk to my mother!"

Stan had already been sniffing around our apartment. So had our landlord, looking for rent, which we hadn't paid in a while, not since Cathy's folks stopped footing the bill. And then there was the band of angry young riot grrrls living upstairs who worshipped at the altar of Ani DiFranco and who'd been calling the cops on us because my gruff and grubby tweaker buddies were walking in and out, lurking about all hours of the night. I had to be fast.

I borrowed Ray's car for the wedding. A Toyota Camry, it had belonged to his parents and was in good shape. No one else in our crew even had a car.

It was Sanger and me, Rhonda and Cathy. I'd gone almost three weeks without speed. I wanted to keep Cathy away from the stuff, plus I thought it important that I be sober for our wedding. But it was a long drive to Nevada, like over three hours. And Sanger's being there meant a lot, and I felt like I owed it to him to get high. Before hitting I-80, we stopped to see Gluehead, who kicked down a sizeable wedding present. Cathy got high, too, which triggered her schizophrenia. By the time we made Reno, she was having a full-blown episode, convinced I was three different people.

"Do you really think I'm three different guys, Cathy?" I asked her.

"Well, I don't think *you're* three different guys," she said.

We got two cheap rooms. I figured I'd sleep with my new wife, and Sanger and Rhonda could share a room. But after the ceremony at the Silver Bells Wedding Chapel, Cathy wouldn't go near me, now convinced I was the devil. I was barely able to get her to say, "I do."

I suppose it was for the best. We didn't have the gas to get back. While Rhonda took care of Cathy, Sanger and I hit the casino. We needed to turn our last $10 into enough scratch to get home. We were lucky. Not only did we win money for gas, we also had cash left over to score an eight ball of crystal meth once we got to San Francisco.

4.
Return to the Land of the Blind

When Amy and I leave the Briarpatch Retreat, we hitchhike to the outskirts of Rutland, where her parents live and her dealer operates. Though I've only known her a week and a half, there is an inextricable connection between us, and what ties us together is not good. Amy and I are bad people who do bad things.

We get a room in a ranch-style motel along the turnpike, between a bait shop and military surplus store. It's an ugly stretch in rural Vermont, with crisscrossed wooden fences and caved-in barns, Harvesters that don't run. You can tell the motel is where local husbands go when their wives kick them out. Hearty sad sacks sit in lawn chairs in front of paint-chipped doors, drinking cheap beer from paper cups, John Deere trucker caps pulled low and shielding shameful eyes, looking extra helpless.

The room smells like body odor and mothballs, the walls are coated with mildew and slime, and the bedspread hasn't been changed since Reagan was in office. Amy makes the call. We pool together the rest of our cash, crumpled up bills that don't amount to much. It only takes half an hour for her guy to show, but it feels like days. We practically throw the money at him, snatch the goods from his hand and push him out the door. We can't unwrap the dope or ourselves fast enough.

I've never fit inside a woman better. By the way her eyes glass over, the sounds she makes as she squirms beneath me, I know that she feels it, too. This is something special. After a prolonged absence, the heroin binds extra hard to our receptors as if to prove a point. Little electrical charges pulsate from her cunt to my cock and back again; it's fusion, osmosis, a nuclear chain reaction. Harder and faster and faster and harder. There is a ferociousness in the yearning. Like sharks thrashing in bloody water after chum.

Normally heroin kills your sex drive, makes it difficult for a man to get it up or maintain an erection. This is not happening with Amy. After I come, I stay hard, and we keep right on fucking. When we pass out from exhaustion and reawake, I'm still hard inside her, and we start back up. We do this all night long.

In the morning, we walk old country roads to get her car, a beat-up, old, red Subaru she's been storing at her folks' house. It's a Saturday, so her parents could be home, and we try to be careful they don't see us. When we start the car, we have to let it idle for a while because it is so cold. No one comes out the house. So either they're not home, or they don't care.

We drive down to Connecticut and my mom's condo. We fix the rest of our dope in the complex's cul-de-sac. My mother is not happy to see I've left rehab again. I tell her I need money to get back to California and then I will leave her alone. She takes one look at the junkie girl I've got nodding out on my arm and grabs her purse. She gives me $500, tells me to leave and never come back.

Amy and I buy more heroin in Hartford. We buy a lot of it. Then we're on I-84, dipping down to 80, heading west.

It's the start of a great road trip. We like the same music; we like the same bands: Tom Waits, Johnny Thunders, Springsteen, Flogging Molly and the Replacements. We like the same authors: Kerouac and Salinger, Vonnegut and Carver. We shoot up constantly in-between the fucking. We fuck in roadside motels, at rest stops, in restaurant bathrooms and gas station johns, in the back seat, the front seat, anywhere with enough room for her to turn around and me to slip my dick out.

By Illinois, we are out of dope.

By Colorado, we are both going into withdrawal. I tell Amy, while she drives and I close my eyes to try to sleep, that we need to drive straight through to San Francisco. Heroin dealers have hours, too, and all the ones I know stop dealing after ten o'clock at night.

I wake in Denver, in a slum off Laramie Street, in the middle of the night to find Amy shaking with the cold fits.

We have $60 left. This isn't much concern because we've found a way to make money while on the road. Hitting truck stops throughout the Midwest, Amy puts on a short skirt, affects a sultry pout and solicits the married men when they go inside to pay for their gas. (We'd later try this once inside SF city limits and it would prove useless anywhere other than the Midwest.)

We drive up, down, and around the streets of Laramie, stopping every hooker and bum we see at late-night check cashing places or 24-hour donut shops, asking if they know where to cop dope. An hour later, all we can find is crack. Desperate to shoot something, we score some rock, which I break down in vinegar. Unlike heroin or amphetamines, crack does not break down in water; you have to use either lemon juice or vinegar, which scorches the hell out of your veins. It is very good crack, but as any dope fiend can tell you, shooting coke when you can't find heroin is about the worst idea you can have, the warm sedation of opiate euphoria replaced by the amped-up cold jitters of cocaine. It is during this increasingly uncomfortable stretch that we meet Doug E. Fresh.

Doug E. Fresh is just another vagrant at a gas station wrapped in a ripped, padded, blue coat reinforced with duct tape, but he swears he knows where to find the best shit. He is black, maybe fifty-five, sixty years old, refers to himself in the third person, and is obviously strung out on something. We hand over all our money.

In one of his more lucid moments, Doug E. Fresh tells me that he only got hooked on drugs after his son overdosed, because, heartbroken, he "had to understand why." It is a touching story, though it soon occurs to me he might just be a crackhead. In addiction, there is no one quite as sinister or conniving as the crackhead.

While Amy sits in a parked car blocks away, Doug E. Fresh, with our last $40 in pocket, takes me throughout the various projects and skid row haunts of Denver in search of heroin until two in the morning.

The absurdity of the moment doesn't strike me at first. This isn't the first time I have been in a strange city, pinning my hopes on a stranger after dark.

Every time Doug E. Fresh sees a cab driver or whore, he crouches and points a finger. "Hey'ya there, Mac… Hello, Doll, Doug E. Fresh here, keepin' it real," he says, and then he pulls his finger like he's pulling the trigger of a gun.

Doug E. Fresh and I are standing at a pulled window shade or a cracked-open basement door, in plain view should any police drive by, and he whispers, "Hey'ya, Charlie, Doug E. Fresh here, keepin' it real, open the door, got some folks wanna buy some heron." Black people never pronounce the "i" in heroin; it's always "heron," you know, like the bird.

It takes me a while, but I soon realize Doug E. Fresh does not know any of these people; there is nobody inside these homes to sell us a damn thing. These are condemned buildings. Doug E. Fresh is insane. It is two in the morning in Denver, Colorado. I am dopesick, out of money and following the lead of a man who is bat-shit crazy.

I return to the car empty handed, Amy cries, and we drive away. Leaving town, we pass Doug E. Fresh. He sits on the side of the road in a shopping cart. He is cradling a pineapple rind like an infant and barking at the moonlight.

We arrive in San Francisco shortly after ten the next night and can't find shit. We sleep in the car. At least we try to.

Welcome home.

5.
The Boys of Belvedere

People ask how it started, how a good-looking, lapsed Catholic from Connecticut turned into a no-good, thieving junkie, homeless on the streets of San Francisco. But I don't have an answer. I'm not sure that it can be pinned on anger and alienation alone, a dad who may've been better suited for another line of work. I think I may've read too many books. Mostly I believe it comes down to this: I asked for more than this world could give back.

As for where it began in San Francisco, though, that's easy. A house on Belvedere Street.

I named the painting *The Boys of Belvedere*, modeling its composition on an old photograph of the Beats, the one where Kerouac has his arms around a very young Ginsberg and Burroughs. I think Hal Chase is also in that picture. I worked in oils, layering deep burgundies, black-blues, faded umbers and ochres, trying to mimic the lurid feel of old pulp fiction covers, *Fast and Loose*, *Sin on Wheels*, *Confessions of Teenage Hit Man*, that sort of thing. I used to cart my easel and brushes everywhere I went. It was during a brief span where I thought I might be a painter.

I met the Boys of Belvedere when I answered an ad in the *SF Weekly* looking for a singer. I'd had a pretty big band in Connecticut. At least, I thought it was big. We were paid a few hundred bucks to play in bars, had been interviewed on a local college radio station. We were even slated for a show at the legendary punk club CBGBs in

NYC, before I broke up the band and pulled up stakes, looking to be a bigger fish in a bigger pond somewhere far away. Everyone I met in San Francisco can be traced back to that house. 23 Belvedere.

There was John Wayne Newton and Riley and Ben and Dan Jewett, whose band, The Creeping Charlies, I was singing in. Then there was Luke Preacher and Dave 2 and Johnny Christ. There was also Brian Fast. Or rather, the stories about Brian Fast. These were not good stories.

There were girls at Belvedere, as well. Like Kerrie, the stripper who was married to John Wayne Newton. They'd met while she was dancing at Regal World, whose slogan was "Where You Are King." (That's how John Wayne would ask for the number when he called Information. He'd say, "May I please have the number for Regal World, where I am king?") And there was Rachel and Brenda, and Daphne and Gwen, both of whom Dan chased after tirelessly. Gwen went on to marry a big shot Hollywood movie star.

I wasn't so interested in the girls though, except for Kerrie. I mean, they were pretty and smelled nice and I liked that, and I liked fucking them, sleeping with them, waking up next to them, but I was after something deeper than girls. I found it with the Boys of Belvedere.

Hopped up on amphetamines and Jim Beam, the Boys were all artists—writers, filmmakers, musicians—misfits basically, but misfits who believed they could leave their lasting creative mark on this world. When Hemingway was living as an expatriate in Paris in the '20s, he wrote how lucky he felt to be in a city teeming with such raw artistic possibility. That's how I felt about San Francisco and the Boys of Belvedere—like something important was going to happen. This was our moveable feast.

When I got there in 1992, Riley was enduring a brutal stretch of abstinence, not by choice. Going without any for thirteen months will do strange things to a man. Ben was Sancho Panza to Riley's Don Quixote. Both had recently graduated from film school and were working on a screenplay, a road picture, in which they wanted me to star. I would play the lead: Ether Plimpton.

John Wayne Newton was my favorite, though, which is why I couldn't sleep with his wife, even as she chased me all over the city. Once I woke in the middle of the night and found Kerrie sleeping next to me. She'd crawled up my fire escape, two stories, through an open window and into my bed. When I asked her what she was doing there, she said she thought I needed milk. I never touched her.

The Boys all played together in a funk band called the Groove Pigs. I hated the band and the name, but a greater bunch of guys you couldn't ask for (except for Joe; he was an arrogant prick).

I had a good paying job back then, in charge of the entire bindery and shipping departments at a South Bay print shop. I even had my own business card. I was good with numbers. I'd moved to San Francisco with my hometown girlfriend, but we'd done nothing except fight since arriving on the West Coast and had recently broken up after I caught her screwing around on me. Wasn't the first time, wouldn't be the last.

A subversive frat house that forever smelled like a hard, funky cheese, 23 Belvedere was a meeting place and launching pad for good times. After work, I'd head there, leave my nice shoes in the car and walk up those stairs knowing I could always find someone up for something.

The third-floor flat was falling apart, and though its decrepit physical state—the kicked-out banister rungs and fire-scorched walls, upholstery that reeked of moist, dirty feet, vomit on the ceiling—would prove not that dissimilar from the bowery rooms I'd soon call home, there was a world of difference back then.

23 Belvedere was wild summer nights and yearbook antics, a place where guys got so drunk they puked in their hands just to see how high they could throw it.

Where my addiction would lead me, skid row at the Royan and 16th Street Hotels, nobody was laughing in those places. I would be alone there, waiting to die.

Sitting at the 500 Club, I was on a really boring date, one of those nights where no matter how much you drink, you can't seem to get drunk. Elle was the daughter of one of the guys I worked with, Sam. My cushy gig in middle management at the print shop made me a lot of money, and I was good at my job, but I was a kid. I didn't have any idea what I wanted to do with my life. I just knew this wasn't it.

I had the beginnings of a serious problem with alcohol, a developing one with speed, and I definitely wasn't satisfied. The only thought that sustained me was this: Each morning on my drive to work, I'd come to the 101/280 split and think how maybe, one day, I would keep going, all the way to New Mexico or Arizona, where I could find work as a ranch hand and bunk in a barn, the southwestern sun drenching me in hot, white light, desert winds washing me clean at night as I bedded down on prairie dirt and wrote poems about dark-skinned girls named Angeline. Maybe I'd fall in love with a trapeze artist when the carnival came to town and go on the road. Who knew? In two years, I could be stowing away on steamboats, hopping trains for grand adventures, picking red wine grapes in some exotic countryside. It was the possibility that kept me from driving off the edge.

I knew Elle liked me, and there was no reason for me not to like her. She was pretty and nice. But I was bored with pretty, and I was sick of nice. The girl was lulling me to sleep. Not even midnight, I was fighting to stay awake.

Then the Boys of Belvedere walked in.

That night everything was possible. We were young and wild and mad. John Wayne Newton led an expedition to North Beach, where we all beat off in private booths in front of live nude girls before climbing atop limousines and howling into the night. We drank until we could barely stand and talked about the things in life that truly matter: picking up girls and playing music and getting fucked up.

We slummed the out-of-the-way grottos and secret bars with Tiki motifs and umbrella drinks; and I kept silent that I am actually Sal Paradise. We were the lions and nobody sleeps. We hit Little Buddha and stared into one another's eyes to convey an unspoken camaraderie, an intensity that cannot be measured in words.

We got high and listened to music, and John Wayne and I giggled like schoolgirls each time we heard Liz Phair sing the word "fuck." I was flying ten million light years from the Earth and never will I feel closer to home.

We inhaled bus fumes and wrote our names in piss on the sides of churches, picked fights in the Latino Mission and counted rats in empty lots. We all dressed up in dusty blue, polyester wedding suits and vandalized public property, and we were unstoppable. We wrote. We wrote about beauty and truth and love and madness, and it will never taste sweeter than it did that night.

That night we all got laid. Even Riley.

We were in an apartment on Halloween, on a rooftop with a birdcage, and everyone was singing and passing out on fire escapes, the cityscape panoramic, and look! Somebody tied Johnny Christ to a telephone pole, naked, again.

And then, the barbecue plummeted from its perch, startling us out of our drug-induced slumber, as it crashed from the top deck of the houseboat to the soundtrack of our lives and *Frank's Wild Years*, before splashing soundlessly into Lake Havasu.

That night was one long, cross-country trip through Las Vegas.

■

I read books. I saw plays. I took apart tape decks. I drank a lot of alcohol. I did a lot of drugs. I was 23 years old. I'd work my insignificant day job in that little print shop, but the nighttime was mine. John Wayne Newton and me. Johnny Christ and me. Dan Jewett and me. All of those boys and me.

That was how it was then, over the first couple summers at least, before the drugs went from an afterthought to the only thought. Sunny Saturdays on the roof of my Fair Oaks apartment, surveying the packed cars of the Mission and seafarer homes of Bernal Heights, freed up for whatever this world wanted to one day throw my way. Dan and I would sit up there and strum our guitars and write our songs and drink our Tecates, and there didn't seem to be a good reason why this life couldn't get better. Those were the days of billowy clouds and sunshine, the days of Methedrine and roses. I was 3,000 miles from home. I started doing speed more and sleeping less. My philosophy then: *While you are sleeping, other people are having fun.*

The bars beneath the glow of holy streetlights, the subway that could take you there, the all-night rap sessions conducted from the darkest hearts in the kindest boys. And the music. We'd play all night and into the day, and every once in a while, it'd happen. We'd play back recordings of four-piece instrumentals and hear six. We weren't crazy. They were there. Ghosts on the train. Ghosts on the bandwagon. Ghosts inside the walls and on the floors and in our hearts. I heard them, and if I had any evidence remaining of their existence, you'd hear them too.

I thought it would never end, that I could walk on bonfire beaches and climb radio towers, cruise that coastline forever. I was in love. It's a love I'll never find again, no matter how long or hard I search. I loved everything. I was loved by everybody. I could close my eyes and tiptoe on the sun, spin a thousand times and have every bud blooming with the piquancy of wildflowers and sulfur.

The bartenders all knew my name, and they poured 'em strong, and I'd wake up under a check-in desk at the Marriott at two in the morning, stumble out and up Market Street and into a sex club to talk to a teased-out, bleached blonde in a booth for $5, and oh the way she'd smile, the adorable, precious sex-kitten phrases she'd mouth... Black slapped so hard on night, it overlapped the day that slivered in as I cooked breakfast with my own pans, and it didn't make a damned bit of difference the drugs I did the night before, because I could still smoke my cigarettes and listen to Mark Curry and Hell's House Band, and I'd eat my sourdough toast, splash a little bourbon into freshly squeezed orange juice, and I'd set that stubborn course right.

We'd find our way. We'd taken our hits, and now we would watch the seasons change in our favor.

We were the Kodak moment of the perfect blowjob: that timeless moment where everything ceases to exist except your dick and her lips and the sweet sounds of sucking. And just as you orgasm... Boom! A bluebird is sitting on a telephone wire, and she is singing the softest lullaby, and it's springtime in the city.

And whose car is this anyway? And where are we going? Can we even cross state lines? What was her name?

Grab a slice of pizza and let's do a couple lines, and then she'll play you your favorite song on her grandmother's piano before taking you to bed.

Write it all down now, because tomorrow, boys, it will be gone.

6.
Church

I've never seen a rain like this. The downpour started as soon as I left the church and has been following me since.

There is a drop-in at the old church on 19th and Dolores in the Mission, where they feed us day-old pastries, serve a hot meal, and show Clint Eastwood movies. Today we had fish sticks and watched *The Outlaw Josey Wales*. I would never set foot in a goddamn church otherwise. But it's later now. The dull red brick of the church has been replaced with the homeboy low riders of the ghetto, and I am in Hunter's Point, parked in a 40-foot mobile home in an abandoned lot behind *Thrasher Magazine*, sitting next to a pit bull runt named Rip-off.

"I knew my life was going nowhere," Les says, "when I was seventeen and going to get a tattoo of a target here." He points to the inside of his elbow.

Les robbed a Hostess truck, and we are eating cherry pies for lunch. The trailer belongs to Gluehead, and he lets Les stay in it for free. Glue and Les go way back. Glue and I don't speak much anymore, not since I became a full-time heroin addict. I hear he's moving down the coast to Pacifica. It's only Les and me and my girlfriend, Amy, who are here today.

It's been two months since Amy and I met in a Vermont rehab, since we hit the open road and I brought her to my San Francisco.

The honeymoon is over.

We fight all the time. She makes me so mad, I'll scream at her like my father used to my mother. I've found a way to mimic his pitch. I am not as big as he, but it's still intimidating. I can see it scares her. It also makes her shut up. It is not a good character trait, I know.

I'm not sure of the day. Feels like a Wednesday. Days and dates don't matter much for people like us. Everything I own fits in this backpack. It is maroon and ripped; it's where I keep my needles and burnt spoon, my empty heroin bags to scrape in tough times. It's where I used to keep my toothbrush, too. But I lost it. I don't have very good hygiene.

Broken bicycle parts, insulation, and torn couch cushions pin me in a corner, knees against chest. The trailer is stuffed to capacity with speed freak salvage. There is no electricity today; Les forgot to turn on the generator. Amy is passed out, next to Rip-off, who twitches in his doggy dreams, and I envy him. Our lives aren't that dissimilar to a dog's. We both scavenge for food, will eat pretty much anything; we both sleep on the ground. We lack the ability to communicate with humans.

A dank gray filters through the heavily clad windows as the bay whips its filthy, leaden wind over the garbage dump where we are parked, rattling the thin shell of the camper with a sea salt whistle you can almost taste.

Amy and I walk from Hunter's Point up to Noe Valley. Her car broke down a few days ago near the music studio off 3rd Street. We pushed it into the parking lot, where it should be safe until we can kick down some dope for a junkie mechanic to take a look. It's not like we can have AAA tow it to an auto shop. It's a long walk in the rain, but we don't have the dollar apiece for the bus.

We can't be late for work.

Amy and I are part of a racket stealing money from banks in supermarkets. It's a dangerous job, but it pays well. What choice do we have? Heroin isn't like other drugs. Getting high isn't an option. You don't get high, and your body will not function.

We huddle in a doorway to keep out of the cold fog that tumbles over Twin Peaks, rolling like an avalanche down the mountain where the giant radio tower looms, blinking though the dreariness, a guiding light to lost sailors on a stormy night.

Amy and I are waiting for Tom Pitts.

There are a lot of Toms in our group, so we have to give them nicknames. There's Big Tom and Little Tom, Evil Tom, and of course Tom Pitts. Tom Pitts is my best friend and a rare breed: a reliable doper. He had a pretty big band in the '80s, Short Dogs Grow. He drives a cab these days.

The first time I met Tom Pitts was at Hepatitis Heights. He stopped by after his graveyard shift. He's an old friend of Sailor Mick, who runs the shooting gallery. Sailor Mick is insane and thinks he is a millionaire. He claims to have "T-bills" stashed all over the world and says one day he is going to cash them in and live in style on a beach in the tropics. Each T-bill is worth $10,000, he says. Despite his millions, any time I've been at Hepatitis Heights, Sailor Mick never has his own cigarettes or lighter. I don't live there anymore. But when I did, on the few occasions Mick actually had money, the worst thing you could do was borrow any of it. If you borrowed $3 from Sailor Mick, the next day he'd be running around town telling everyone you owed him six grand.

When Tom Pitts came over that first time, it was five in the morning. We'd been up all night, pounding cottons and scraping bags, trying to stave off the sickness. It's an awful moment for a junkie, seeing the morning light come and knowing you don't have the means to get well.

My first thought when I saw the guy was what a wreck he was—ashen, gaunt, with fine brown hair that looked like it'd been dusted with flour, cuts and sores lining his lips. Tom kicked down dope and got us well that morning. After knowing him for a month, I remember thinking that he didn't look so bad.

I learned early that you could trust Tom Pitts with your dope. He'd make sure you get your rightful share of any given deal.

Tom brings us up to the house where we pick up the checks.

Tom knows a pair of speed dealers, this dork with coke-bottle glasses, Ralphie, and his girlfriend, Wanda, a pug-nosed brut with a prison mentality and Hep C, who are masterminds of a scam involving phony checks and bank fraud. Ralphie and Wanda employ a team of tweakers who dumpster dive for them. That is what speed freaks call their midnight scavenging trips, leaping into industrial trash bins, headfirst to the bottom, sifting through used rubbers and wet coffee grounds like they're snorkeling for pearls. Diving in the Financial District, the tweakers look for financial documents, anything with bank account numbers on it, which they bring back to Ralphie and Wanda in exchange for drugs. Wanda then creates payroll checks on her computer, scanning in the bank's name and logo and trying to guess the next feasible sequential number, which is not an exact science. There is an endless parade of junkies willing to cash these checks. All you need is a legitimate photo ID and no concern for your future. All profits split, 50/50.

Amy and I have been doing this job for the past couple weeks, and it's a decent payday every time we do. Except that it's never enough. That's the problem with junk. Money doesn't last. Like Tom Pitts says: it wouldn't matter if heroin cost a penny; it'd just mean we'd have bigger habits.

There are many drawbacks and potential pitfalls to this scam. One, the check can't be for more than $800, because that bumps the crime up into a much more severe category. So every check is for around $798, which alone invites scrutiny, all these derelicts walking into your bank trying to cash checks for the same amount. And addicts need to squeeze every last cent, so you can forget about Wanda printing up some for less. Two, you can't hit the same bank more than once, for obvious reasons. Three, it is only a matter of time until you are caught. The nice part is, if a bank grows suspicious, they usually don't call the cops right away. They'll say they are keeping your ID, and if you put up a fight, they'll *suggest* calling the cops to sort it out, at which point you get the hell out of there.

But even that is a stall tactic, because you can't keep cashing checks that aren't real.

7.
Brian Fast

I met Gluehead through Brian Fast. B. Fast.

Brian was a founding member of the Boys of Belvedere. That's where I first encountered the name anyway. By the time I got there, he had fallen out of favor with most of the group, his drug addiction and antics taking him far beyond what polite society is willing to tolerate, and so he rarely came around. At Belvedere, Brian Fast soon became a bad memory, a spook story to serve as a warning to kids like me who were having too good of a time.

"Watch it, man, or you'll end up like Brian!"

Oksana was boiling cat heads in a big pot on the stove when I got back to the apartment. Oksana collected roadkill, cooking off the fur and using the bleached bits of skull as jewelry. A homeless, teenaged speed dealer, she'd race the midnight streets of San Francisco on her skateboard, a demon pixie draped in shiny beads and necklaces delivering product, two giant guard dogs snapping at her side like the Hounds of Hell. I'd lost my job at the print shop and was living on unemployment, banished from my two-bedroom home in the hills of Diamond Heights, cast down to the bowels of the Mission. It didn't take long for Oksana and me to start sleeping together, and for her and her dogs to move into my apartment. With me and Brian, that is.

The five of us shared a one-room studio on 18th Street the size of your average kitchen. Brian Fast did not like Oksana.

Brian and I had become friends. I think that's what you'd call it. I'd invited him to move into my place after his wife kicked him out and he had nowhere else to go. Even though I'd been warned and should've known better, I couldn't help but find the guy captivating. As I did more and more speed, the Boys of Belvedere wanted less and less to do with me, until, like Brian, they didn't want me around at all. So the two exiles banded together. Like Ratso Rizzo to Joe Buck, Brian took me under his wing to show me how an addict stays alive: how to use manipulation and take a person's inherent goodness and generosity and use it against him to get what you wanted. And Brian Fast always got what he wanted.

Once Brian and I were walking in the middle of night, the streets silent, the city asleep. We passed a parked car. On the front seat were two unopened packs of Camel cigarettes. Brian picked up a nearby brick, smashed the window and took the cigarettes. After we'd run and were safely away, he said, "I wouldn't have done that if there was only one pack. But two unopened packs? Why should they have two when I have none?" That is how Brian Fast approached everything, as if the world itself was his birthright.

Brian Fast always had an agenda. He saw it as his sworn duty to attack everything in this life that contained the slightest hint of convention or decency. You didn't like Brian? Good! He thrived on your being uncomfortable. Brian used to say that there are all sorts of unspoken pleasantries to which people adhere: you don't take the last piece of crumb cake; you at least offer to get the bill; you do not kick a dog when he's down. Well, if Brian were in your kitchen when the pizza man arrived, you wouldn't expect him to chip in on the pie. He'd be too busy eating the last piece of strudel while kicking the living shit out of your sick dog.

When you have no semblance of community, when you write your own ticket governing etiquette, when you find a way to shake loose from the confines of manners that pigeonhole the rest of mankind, new avenues become available. And Brian was a master at exploiting these.

Brian Fast always got what he wanted, because Brian Fast always made sure he won the battle of who cares less.

He was original, though. You had to give him that.

Brian said we didn't even need meth, that there's a nerve in the back of our necks we could sever and never have to sleep again. He swore he had a transistor radio implanted in his head. The aliens put it there back when he was 95 pounds and working as a bus driver. But even he'd grown suspicious of its messages, the things it would tell him to do, the voices in his head that were not his own. Brian claimed he could see souls, cylindrical tubes in the chest cavity, running left shoulder to right hip. Brian didn't like it when people said "ironic." He said there is no such thing as irony; irony is a literary term involving heroes and fate. Brian said there are no real heroes. Brian didn't believe in using semi-colons either. He was lit up on detergent.

Brian first told me about the radio they implanted in his head when he got back from Alaska. His wife, soon to be ex, had sent him there to work on a fishing boat while she moved out his things. When he returned, he was worse than ever, shoveling in speed at an incomprehensible clip to make up for lost time. He began furiously taking apart tape decks, which by itself was no big deal. He'd taken apart tape decks before. We all did. It's what speed freaks do, dismantling the internal wirings and mechanisms, trying to understand how the drives and motors inside make it work. But it was different now. In a blackened back room, Brian would huddle over circuit boards, soldering gun in hand, smoking crank, not eating, not sleeping, inhaling heavy metals, goading night into bleeding daylight.

After his wife gave up on him, whatever good Brian Fast may've had left, however buried, was gone forever. Frequency and pitch became all that mattered to him. Brian had become obsessed with making these home recordings culled from tweaked-out jam sessions with Glue and Sanger at the shack that he'd taped on a boombox, adding overdubs onto a gutted Tascam 4-track portable mixer. He removed all but mid-range from his guitar, adding vocals by singing into the ears of headphones, whose polarity could be redirected, thus turning them into a microphone and making it sound like you were in a tiny telephone booth, somewhere underwater and very far away. The shitty lo-fi quality of these efforts would've put the hippest indie rocker to shame.

This is how we lived, nobody sleeping in our claustrophobic apartment, that wigged-out, slimy tweaker vibe saturating the air, worming through our skin. While I drew cartoons in a corner, Brian worked on his crappy recordings, glowering with malice at little Oksana, who only wanted to boil her dead cats and make pretty jewelry.

A low growl from the dogs was all that kept him from murder.

My tutelage under Brian Fast led me to the Dark Side. I became a willing pupil of his wicked teachings because I did not want to play by the same set of rules as everyone else. I wanted exceptions made for me, and Brian Fast would show me how to make that happen.

I remember complaining to Brian once that the thing I hated most about doing speed was the come down. His response still buzzes inside my head: *"Man, we don't ever have to come down..."*

And I wouldn't for a long, long time.

8.
The City

The early morning light spreads through the makeshift curtains and onto Pinkle's partially paralyzed left arm that he's poking at like a voodoo doll stuck rag. Cars race up Fell Street, maintaining their swift speed from the highway off-ramp. Old and dull points lie across cardboard box furniture draped with bandanas, and dried blood is speckled on the mirror and ceiling, our own private libertine constellation. The television replays the scenes we know all too well. These are the good times.

The Casa Loma is a transient hotel, with brownish-red stains on the mattress and curtains ripped from old bed sheets tacked to the windows. It is one of the places we stay when we get enough money, when we are able to get out of someone else's trailer, away from the shooting gallery on the hill. The water here works, and there is a functioning toilet and shower down the hall. For people like us, the Casa Loma is about as good as it gets. It's the Top of the fucking Mark.

Amy and I have been hanging around with Pinkle a lot lately. I met Pinkle through Tom Pitts, who doesn't like him much. Pinkle is a gimp. He says he fell off a ladder and that is why he has the metal rods fused into the bones of his upper spine, which abnormally cranes his neck forward like a glorious fried bird, his left arm all but useless. Tom says Pinkle didn't fall off any ladder; he nodded out from doing too much dope and it wore his vertebrae thin.

Pinkle recently discovered the joys of speedballing. He has a $300,000 trust fund. He's my new best friend.

It's 7 a.m. and we've just copped. Amy is worthless twenty-three and a half hours a day. She is a horrible human being. I love her.

I use the mirror and hold my breath, puffing out my jugular, which I've just discovered. I can't believe I haven't tapped this resource sooner. Once you get past the willies of jabbing a needle into your neck, you've got two, maybe three months before she's going to dry up. I register, pull the plunger back, extra carefully—you don't want an abscess here—and I'm in.

But we can't rest, because the high never lasts as long as you'd like. As soon as a junkie shoots up, he's on the lookout for his next fix.

Check out time. We gather our belongings, wrap ourselves in wool and canvas sacks, tie bands around our greasy heads and put plastic bags over our feet. Like nomads, we make our exodus from the fruitless in search of the plenty.

An addict spends a lot of time waiting—waiting for the hustle to come together, waiting for the dealer to show, waiting for the sickness to come. Waiting sucks. And waiting on money is the worst. Until we get money, we can't get high. Until we get high, we are trapped in your world.

Too many junkies have been getting popped lately, so Ralphie and Wanda have issued a moratorium on the check scam until the heat dies down. Tom Pitts says to keep cool; they'll start up again. But until they do, it's panhandling at the BART, snatching tips from sidewalk eateries, or waiting for Pinkle to access his trust, which, as it turns out, is in the hands of an executor who knows what a scumbag he is and doesn't make getting any of it easy.

Syd Barrett's "Baby Lemonade" is playing in Muddy Waters, the coffee shop where we wait, like the soundtrack to a Wim Wenders film, a cast of oddball extras boasting San Francisco eccentricities coloring the room: the old man with the bushy, white beard playing checkers with his little dog; the two industrial goths, painted in black latex, steel chains for earrings connected to their nose, talking earnestly about platform shoes; the fat hippy-dippy lady wrapped in a muumuu and rainbow shawl, stack of newspapers on a hand truck, tearing up over a headline about global warming.

Pinkle is wheezing. Amy won't look at me.

Outside, it's a torrential rain—*the church rain*—come back to follow me once again. I step outside for a cigarette and can almost see the Roxie movie house around the corner at 16th and Valencia, next door to the Mediterranean food stand where my brother Billy and I used to eat lamb kebobs and shawarma wraps when he flew out to visit, back when I still worked and had my own apartment, back when I was the sort of big brother he could look up to.

The clouds churn and burble like an angry European sky. I listen to the rhythmic patter of raindrops, catching, dripping off awnings and signposts. Rainy season. The lonesome sound spinning tires make on asphalt, the slick creaking of opening and closing wet metal doors, the howl and shiver of the Pacific Northwest. I flick my cigarette into the gutter and go back inside.

The café is decorated in that sassy SF style. Shitty paintings of ugly hats hang on large canvases, covering the walls, all different kinds of hats, like a cracked-out Dr. Seuss picture book, bright symmetrical blotches deliberately splashed outside the lines, garish and obnoxious. The girl behind the counter has a tattoo of a dragon slapped across the exposed top of a large breast and several piercings. I've wanted to ask her for a cup of water for over an hour now but have been too intimidated. She isn't completely unattractive, her shaggy brown hair pushed back by a headband that reads "Fuck You Too."

■

I blame Jack Kerouac.

I was nineteen and backpacking through Europe with a friend. We were on a train somewhere in Northern Italy, coming back from Greece, headed for Germany. It was just after the wall came down. A summer of standing-room-only in sleeper cars, warm cherry jelly, stale baguettes and chocolate bars.

I'd picked up Kerouac's *Lonesome Traveler* in a bookstore in Venice, the first time I'd read him. It made me daydream about becoming a merchant marine or mountain ranger and disappearing into the stars. I gazed out the window, at the sun-bleached Italian hillside racing by, the unfathomable history of the Mediterranean on the other side, overwhelmed by the prospect of having my whole life ahead of me.

Up until this trip and that book, I'd been aimless, a slacker failing out of college, wasting afternoons drinking beer and playing whiffle ball at my part-time job for the town's Community Center, pinning my hopes on a band making it big by rocking weekends at a bar called The Cool Moose, and all the while, in the back of my mind, I was terrified I'd get stuck married to some townie, whose ass would continue to swell long after the babies came, as I wasted away in a soul-sucking 9-to-5 at the paper mill, counting the minutes until I died.

But now I had a direction. And I knew where I'd go.

Kerouac's San Francisco.

The line that did it stays with me. Jack is on a train, spiriting the wretched heat of SoCal for the cool, welcoming fog of the Bay. He can't shake his dead father's ghost or the sins ravaging his bones. But the liquor is hitting him right, and the cigarettes taste good, and who knows how tomorrow will turn out or whose bed he'll end up in tonight...

Late night juke joints, bottles of port, North Beach sex clubs and free love, before spending six months alone atop a mountain where your only job is to eat beans from a can and report the occasional forest fire. It would be poetry readings and coffee huts and bongo drums and pretty girls (who by the way really *do* make graves). Longshoreman work, train conductor work, hanging out with the sleepy jazz musicians during the day, slumming it with the madmen on the bowery at night. It called me out.

I strapped on my guitar and headed west.

I woke to a car horn honking in a dark driveway, grabbed my duffel bag and bounded down the steps. I tossed the few personal items I was taking with me—some mixed tapes, a week's worth of clean clothes, toothbrush—into the backseat of my girlfriend's car. I clutched my book to my chest. My mom said to be careful as she dried the tears from her eyes. And we were on our way.

We stopped overnight in Missouri to see my girlfriend's long-lost stoner dad, then decided to take the southern route to see America. We dipped into Texas, and I watched the sky open up, the clouds spilling over one another like desperate drunken lovers, mountains expanding indefinitely across endless horizons. I was twenty-one years old. What isn't possible driving through Texas on your way to California when you're twenty-one? Cat Stevens on the radio, taking turns on the bottle of red wine purchased half a state over, window down, singing along, chain-smoking cigarettes. I was leaving home, and for the first time, I was free, the kind of free you will only be once; I wasn't too young to know that.

And I owed it all to Jack. Jack Kerouac was the real America, the America that I wanted to get to know, that spirit of endless possibility, the America that exists only in the dreams of twenty-one-year-old boys as they hit the wide-open expanse of western Texas, in the mystery that winds through the stark New Mexican desert and rises up to greet the wild, star-laden Arizona night. Cheap cups of coffee and no one knows your name. "Where ya headed, son?" "Hey, man, it's all the same." All-night diners, drifters with no past, poets scribbling down ideas on napkins, and honey-haired waitresses you want to ask to marry you as they refill your cup. I had heard it all, I had read it all, and *now I wanted it to be mine.*

From there on out, I swore every time I saw a girl in a too-tight waitress smock, tits-popping-out-of-her-dress, America, I'd make the most out of my short time on God's green earth.

That's how I got here.

More than the drugs, this city is what keeps me tethered to this life. There is nothing quite like that feeling you get from a Friday night in San Francisco. Impossibly too-cute girls, wisps of hennaed hair hanging down in Japanese kitten eyes, thrift store garb and funky two-toned shoes, walking in pairs, sugary smack tandem, bubble gum fluorescent lipstick to die for.

Police chase the homeless from their cardboard box homes in the alleyways behind McDonald's and the 16th Street BART station entrance.

"Outfits!"

"You lookin'?"

Computer programmers and the bio-tech kids up from San Mateo and Foster City, Silicon Valley hotshots hitting the all-night dance spots and slick Guerrero Street bars, scarfing burritos and copping a taste of inner-city life.

"One 'n' ones!"

"You buyin'?"

I watch the Maximas and Volvos circle the block, trying to snag a late night parking space, hot fumes rising off the street with the hopes of the hopeless, the dreams of the dreamers, last call for the hipsters.

Bums have set up old toasters, books, cassette tapes, baseball caps, pants that nobody wants, single shoes, stuff salvaged from the trash propped up pretty on spread out blankets infested with scabies, everything on sale for a dollar. The lights from the night sky fuse with the lights from the restaurant interiors, the apartments and bars, the headlights from cars. I had forgotten how big and bright this place could be.

The Mariachis are marching and singing in Spanish harmony, and the hobos keep asking if I have any change to spare. (Sanger says, "Spare change, what's that? Money I don't need?") You can smell the enchiladas and taste the desperation. A film noir, *Detour*, is playing on a double bill tonight, part of this year's Festival at the Roxie, where they offer yeast instead of butter to sprinkle on organic popcorn and a wide selection of teas. A greasy kid with greasy dreads and a ripped Dinosaur Jr. jacket is posing outside the Albion, beat-up guitar case collecting crumpled dollar bills. It all feels so perfect.

Maybe I have money in my pocket. I may even have a wife who still loves me somewhere, a home, a future. All I know for sure is that, right now, I don't feel so alone.

I scan the street, 16th, 17th, let my eyes caress the sharp angles and graceful curves of the cafés and taquerias, imbibing the robin's egg blue, inhaling burnt sienna and cotton candy pink. Like a specter caught in the holy lights, I trace the telephone lines and wires, tumble through tenement windows, slither beneath bed sheets, across rooftops and down clotheslines.

I try to gather up everything I know, everything that I have learned since I began plugging myself into God's colorful celebration. I think I might be onto something here...

Then it's gone. And I feel myself slipping off the curb, into the cracks.

9.
My Summer Job

Some kids work on a ranch in Colorado and get to care for a horse named Durango. Others go to Alaska and work on a fishing boat in between semesters at State (or while their wives are moving out all their shit). My summer job was shooting up Gluehead.

When you are an addict, jobs don't get much better than this.

It was a good summer, even though a lot was starting to go wrong. I'd lost my wife after her parents temporarily won the custody battle, committing her to a mental hospital in Minnesota. I was technically homeless, but it wasn't the bad kind of homeless. I still had several music studios where I could crash, a trailer or two under the freeway where they'd let me kick down for a spot on the floor. Sometimes I even scored a couch in a regular apartment. It was also my first full summer shooting heroin.

My partnership with Brian Fast had dissolved by this time. It wasn't one thing that drove a wedge between us; rather, it was a culmination. Brian had been caught sleeping with Glue's psychotic girlfriend, Sparkle Plenty, and that got him booted from the Gluehead Army. I still hung around with him, though. On occasion. Until I got married. Then things got weird. It was uncomfortable whenever it was just the three of us in a room. Plus, being an addict wasn't enough for Brian, who always had to find new, more deplorable levels to sink to, fresher kids to recruit and corrupt. I'd still see him around town, in various drug houses or at Martin de Porres, the soup kitchen by the freeway, and we were friendly enough, but there was undeniable tension. I could never put a finger on it.

Just like with the Boys of Belvedere, I was going through another transition. Junkie Jason had turned me onto smack and the needle the winter before. I'd messed around with heroin in the past, but always by smoking or snorting it, sometimes dissolving it in water inside a nasal dropper. It's not like junk was strictly prohibited within the amphetamine-fueled Gluehead Army, but the habit was certainly frowned upon. Mostly because, unlike speed where you just really, really want it, with heroin you fucking need it. Sanger used to say that when you are friends with a junkie, the only time your friend is actually present is about half an hour before the dope shows up— when he's done scamming and has called The Man; while he's still relatively relaxed because his medicine is on the way and he isn't yet planning his next score. I didn't see what the big deal was. I'd been shooting smack for the past few months, and I was still the same guy. It's not like I was going to start hocking everyone's musical equipment. To me, the Gluehead Army's prejudice against junkies was categorically unfair, a gross inequality, offensive as racism. This was the last summer I'd be welcome at the shack.

Some people are blessed with good genes; they are attractive or can throw a ball 95 mph with movement. Some people get bad genes, and they end up short or bald. I've known guys who were able to shoot up into their sixties, veins as plump and juicy as ripe worms after a monsoon. My brother Billy is one of these guys. He's nowhere close to sixty, of course, but he's still able to fix in the same vein on the same wrist that he started on. Others aren't so lucky.

When you pick up the spike, you first target inside your elbows; then it's your forearms, then your biceps. Next you hit the big one inside your thigh that runs all the way down your inner calf to the ankle and foot, which hurts like hell.

Hands and feet are filled with millions of touchy nerves. After that, you have to get creative. You've got the femoral. But that is deep. You've got fingers and toes, but that's excruciating, not to mention almost impossible because of the tiny size. You've got the neck, which supplies the blood flow to your head, and which most people get squeamish about using. You've got your cock, which we've covered. Then it's the hard-to-reach places you can't get to on your own. Making it tougher, you always have to be on the lookout for arteries. Artery blood and vein blood are very different; one's a frothy bright pink, the other a heavy dark red. But you get so sick of drawing up dry that after a while when you hit *any*thing wet and rosy, you take a chance. You make that mistake once, you don't make it again. Hitting an artery is almost as bad as getting tested for Chlamydia. Injecting into muscle, what junkies call "muscling," works for heroin, sort of, but you don't get the rush, and you risk abscesses. With speed it's all *about* the rush, and there are so many under-the-sink chemicals in its manufacture—jet fuel, rat poison, red phosphorous, acetone, gun bluing, ammonia, and God-knows-what-else—I'm pretty sure your muscles would instantly fizzle and shrivel, like salt on a snail. I never tried it. Neither did the speed freaks I knew like Gluehead.

Dealers are people, too. Some have good veins that will last until they are sent to San Quentin. Others, like Glue, need a little help, and they're willing to pay for it.

In the summer of 1997, while my wife was committed to a sanitarium somewhere far away, and I was experiencing my first bout of homelessness on the mean streets of San Francisco, I had a summer job. If a farm in Minnesota would turn out to be the worst job I ever had, this one was the best, the kind of essay material school kids dream about.

Glue paid me a quarter gram of meth for my services, which wasn't much, but like everything else in a capitalistic market, the price was dictated by supply and demand.

True, Glue really needed to be hit, but there were also a lot of guys willing to give it a shot.

I was equipped with a pager, like a doctor. And just like a doctor, I was on call, 24/7. I took my job seriously. I knew how frustrating it must be for Glue. He could have a pound of crystal on him, but nowhere to inject any of it. Like Jake Barnes surrounded by a pack of randy vestal virgins. If your junk doesn't work, what good is it?

Gluehead only had the veins underneath his arms left. Tricky spot. They'd roll, and you really needed new works to get at them, and Glue, like a lot of shooters, had the bad habit of using the same point over and over until its tip was as blunted as the end of a paper clip. This made you miss, which in this particular spot's not good, the armpit rife with bacteria. You had to be sure to disinfect with alcohol first, which few of us ever did, so you were risking endocarditis, basically a dirt sac around the heart that will kill you.

I didn't last long. Like every other job I've ever had, I was fired from this one, too. As the summer nights drew shorter, my heroin problem grew worse, and a quarter gram of speed just wasn't enough to drag me from the other side of town fast enough, especially if I was chasing down smack. Heroin first, speed second, cocaine third, and then the other stuff like food and shelter. That was my hierarchy of needs.

I understood why Glue started using someone else, but it also bothered me that he thought less of me for becoming a junkie.

But I would show them. I wasn't going to let heroin change me. They'd see I could handle my dope, and I'd remain as true blue as ever.

It was one more promise I couldn't keep.

I was running down Mission Street to the pawn shop with my third guitar of the week. Like Johnny Thunders,

I was living on a Chinese rock. The people at the pawn shop never seemed terribly concerned with how a filthy junkie could possibly own so many guitars. They never asked. And I never told. It was your own damn fault if you let me in your music studio. I'd been banned from all but a couple in the city, and for good reason. This time it was a cream-colored Strat knockoff with rosewood neck. Good condition. Figured it'd fetch me $40.

After I copped, I hoped to have the $26 I needed for a room at the Royan Hotel, an SRO shitbag across the way from the 14th Street projects, maybe enough for a slice of pizza too. You can only sleep outside so many nights before you need to wash off the grime.

I looked down on 14th and Valencia and couldn't figure a way out. I had gone too far. Where did everyone go?

Across the street at the urban reservation, ghetto urchins sold their ghetto drugs, huddled in oversized hoodies and baggy jeans, making deals with the twitchy boys and girls who scratched themselves, shirtless, shoeless, offering stolen electronics or blowjobs for a hit. It could've been Saturday. It could've been fucking Christmas for all it mattered. Maybe I had a girlfriend, or someone I was fucking, somewhere. (I know I still had my wife. She'd be coming back soon when the mental hospital would let her go, and she'd run straight back into the arms of her loving husband with the money we'd need to move into Hepatitis Heights.) The only station that came in on the hotel TV was carrying MLB's Game of the Week. The Cardinals versus the Cubs, I think. Green and orange fuzzy figures danced on the split, warbling screen.

I checked my arm to see how it was healing. It was covered with red, open sores, hard, infected bumps around the injection sites. A week earlier, they'd taken a chunk out of Junkie Jason's arm. You could see down to the bone where they gutted the biceps to get the infection out. They sometimes performed the procedure at the needle exchange, in a secret upstairs room, like a back-alley abortion.

A flesh-eating bacterium was going around that summer, the summer of '98, taking out junkies. I'd heard that in addition to the softball-size chunk they removed from her ass, this rocker chick, Belladonna Cyrus, also lost two roommates. They told us all the time that cooking alone wouldn't kill it. It was an epidemic. We were all scared it would get us. Most blamed the government. I had a theory that it mostly affected the junkies who lived under the bridge, because down there, the city sprayed for rats, and maybe some of the pesticide got on the skin or needle. It wasn't *my* theory, exactly. I'd heard it from this guy, Johnny One-Arm. They called him that because he only had one arm; the bacteria got the other. I sometimes scored under the 101/280 on-ramp off Caesar Chavez, formerly known as Army Street, but I wouldn't shoot up down there. I wasn't an animal.

With the cash from the guitar, I did better than expected. I pulled a "bait and switch" on a little Mexican, swapping wadded up ones for the required twenty, which meant free dope; and dope stolen almost always means more than dope earned. But it also meant I wouldn't be able to score on 16th for a while, which was all right with me, since all they had down there was those puny one 'n' ones anyhow, and burning bridges was sorta my thing.

I didn't have a rubber tourniquet, so I had to use my sock to tie off. I had been wearing the same pair for so long they had started to fuse to my skin. As I peeled them from my feet, bits of flesh ripped off with the bloody cotton fibers. My arms were so skinny, the sock easily wrapped around twice, with plenty left to pull. I tugged as tightly as I could, but no veins were showing.

Getting a hit seemed to take longer every time. Sometimes I was successful. Most of the time, I was not.

This time, I hit a capillary in my thumb. Capillaries can only hold so much before they burst. The capillary burst, and my thumb lumped up, like a frozen peanut M&M. I took a piss in the sink.

These dumps never had in-room bathrooms. Bathrooms were communal property down the hall, and who wanted to walk all the way down the hall just to take a piss? So, I pissed in sinks. I ashed on carpets, and I pissed in sinks.

10.
Jail and the Sickness

Usually they don't call the cops. This time they did.

Amy and I had gone to the Safeway on Market and 16th with a $798 check from Ralphie and Wanda. The security inside supermarket banks isn't as tight as it is in regular banks, which is why we usually target them. Up until now, it's been going smoothly, not a bump in the road. I had gone to this particular Safeway a week earlier and didn't have any problems. It was Amy's turn to cash a check. I had been waiting in the parking lot when I saw the cops pull up. We may fight a lot, but she's still my girlfriend. What was I supposed to do? When I ran inside to make sure she was OK, the teller pointed at me and said, "And that asshole was in here last week doing the same damn thing."

At the end of the first day, it's bad, the sweating and hot and cold flashes, the cramps and constant pressure on your intestines, the headache, the bodyache, the everythingache, the feeling like you have to piss every six minutes, but when you try to, you can't. This is what separates heroin from the other drugs, what makes getting off it such a bitch. You can feel it literally being wrenched from your body, like you've been drawn and quartered and your soul is being sucked out, piecemeal through your pores, extracted with tweezers. You will not be sleeping tonight. Nobody is coming to your rescue, so you grit your teeth and wait for the discomfort to really settle in. Your flesh begins to crawl, and then the kicking starts—that's why it's called "kicking," because your legs involuntarily jerk, thigh muscles convulse, hamstrings twitch, calves spasm. And then comes the sweating and incessant yawning, the mouth bones cracking, and now you can't stop shivering. Your only respite is masturbation and hot showers. So you beat off until your dick is raw and the water runs cold.

Somehow knowing the drill doesn't make it any easier, though. Soon, you are zapped of all strength, drained, incapacitated, curled up in a ball, trying to fix your shaky eyes on one steady spot, praying to things that you don't even believe in, bargaining with what's left of your soul for ten precious minutes of sleep. Shitting your pants, vomiting and crying come later. Slowly, *ever so slowly*, each second progressively worse, each moment feeling more unbearable than the last…Not one second can tick by without your being acutely *aware* of it and *feeling* its pain.

Then starts the second day.

One week later, and I am about to get OR'd, released on my own recognizance. It's been as bad a stretch as I can recall. I haven't eaten a thing in days. Every meal in jail is the same: a slab of processed meat-product and two slices of white bread, a mealy apple, warm 2% milk, and a smear of peanut butter in one of those little paper cups, the kind they put pills in. But not in here. In here, your head could be falling off and you'd be lucky to get an aspirin. It was a big deal whenever the trustees came around with these meals, which were packed in white paper sacks and delivered on rolling carts. I gave mine away to inmates who pounced on them like wharf rats on pie crust. I haven't slept much either. This has been my first extended incarceration. The first thing that comes to mind when you think about jail is the horror stories of rape. But half the people in SF County are wadded-up, sick junkies like me, too weak and pathetic to move let alone fuck, and the other half are really tiny immigrants, politely playing cards in a corner. Nobody is sticking his dick in anything.

The district attorney's office sent someone by asking questions about who was behind the check scam. I guess they don't consider me the mastermind type. I told them, thanks, but no thanks. Ralphie and Wanda are a couple tools, and I couldn't care less what happens to them, but only an idiot talks to the cops.

I am still dopesick as I wait for them to open the door and set me free. All I want to do is smoke a cigarette. It is all I can think about. That and having to use the bathroom. My insides are melting from the withdrawal, soupy sediment trying to squirt out my sphincter. Jail is all hurry up and wait, and they have hurriedly corralled us into a giant pen and told us to wait. Through the high-slotted windows, I see that it is dark outside and can smell fresh air for the first time in seven days. It smells wonderful, like car exhaust and the sea.

We have been waiting in this room since noon. I need to use a toilet. I tell this to a correctional officer, who tells me I have two choices: I can use the bathroom and not get released, or I can "shut the fuck up." I decide on the latter and just deal with the slight anal leakage.

I'm listening to guys talk about what a deal they're getting with "two years suspended after ten" (or is it "ten years suspended after two"?). I keep thinking that I don't belong here.

When I get outside, I bum a smoke and promptly throw up after I take the first drag.

This is the part they don't tell you about in the movies. Or in *On the Road*. This is not rock 'n' roll.

You are not William Burroughs, and it doesn't make a damn bit of difference if Kurt Cobain was slumped over in an alleyway in Seattle the day *Bleach* came out. There is no junkie chic. This is not SoHo, and you are not Sid Vicious. You are not a drugstore cowboy, and you are not spotting trains. You are not a part of anything—no underground sect, no counter-culture movement, no music scene, nothing. You have just been released from jail and are walking down Mission Street, alternating between taking a hit off a cigarette and puking, looking for coins on the ground so you can catch a bus as you shit yourself.

Now you are walking up 6th Street and the brothers are calling out, "Welcome to Crack Central, muthafucker!" It is nothing but drab facades and prostitutes bursting out of vinyl halter-tops, mottled skin and maple-ripple cellulite. You walk among the scurrying vermin as police sirens wail and car windows shatter, through the clusters of pockmarked hooligans and spooky skulls sucking off the menthol butts they've scavenged from the gutter, nursing their 40s and lounging in this one big, urban ashtray. See a crack whore peddling an iron. It's not a new iron. It's not a particularly interesting iron, nor is it loaded with fancy features. It's just a regular, plain ol' iron, and you think, "Wow, what a tough sell…"

Empty cups and empty bottles, empty hearts and empty homes. Nobody has a mother out here. Nobody has a past. A past is too inconvenient. You learn not to flinch when the black and whites cruise by. Steam rises from the grates, and the bums in their beaten wheelchairs with their filthy kittens on a string plead for change. A bullet to the brain would be kinder.

You could wonder if derelicts celebrate birthdays or Christmas, and you could wonder how they got here, but you already know the answer. They were on the bus with you. Notions of shooting stars are very fine, indeed.

You do not worry about death. You will not be that lucky. It's not whether you can get away with snatching that purse or that Snapple from the store. It's not whether you can get a state agency to float you food stamps and bus tokens. You can. That's the problem. You will always find a way to steal what you need to keep going. And you can always find someone to feed you, clothe you, pity you. Sometimes they'll even let you sleep on their floor, where you'll get to listen from the bathroom as they fight in the kitchen, and she's screaming, "I don't want that piece of shit in here!"

And so you close your eyes and pray to God that maybe tonight will be the night you won't have to wake up in the morning.

No, they don't tell you about that part.

In the end, though, how you got here isn't that important, because once you're here, you're here for good. Might as well make the best of it.

We could be at Hepatitis Heights, or maybe we're with Pinkle and Amy on top of Tower Records in the parking garage, the cool autumn breeze blowing gently and the San Francisco sun shining bright. Maybe we're at the Casa Loma by ourselves. Maybe we're in the music studio off 3rd Street or in one of the giant green "space toilets" scattered throughout the city, where for twenty-five cents you get twenty minutes to hunt for a vein in private. Maybe we're with Tom Pitts at one of his squats. It doesn't matter where we are, because today, we have money—*lots* of money. Today everybody gets high.

We could be coming off a four-day sick or just getting out of the pen. It doesn't matter, because today, we have drugs. Whatever anyone could possibly want, we've got. Heroin and amphetamines and cocaine. We've got a brand new set of works, too.

Empty the balloon, add a little water, mix up a hit in the spoon, apply flame. All your problems are about to fly away. Tear off a cigarette filter, place the tip of the pencil into the cotton, draw up 2ccs of this, 4ccs of that. Take the alcohol wipe (in theory) and clean the skin.

Pinch a vein in your neck and stick the needle in. Register, watch the blood blast up the head as you pull the plunger back, the dark red sea mingling with the dirty black tar and cleaning solvents...tap, tap, tap...and you're gone.

You don't have to deal with the monotony or meaninglessness of this place. You don't have to deal with the disappointment of things not having turned out quite the way you would've liked. There is no heartbreak for you. Not anymore. No hurt, no loss, no pain. You do not need anyone's approval or validation. You do not need to curb your spending or save your pennies for that trip to get away from it all, because you've already left.

It is as close to God as you will ever get.

11.
Close Calls

It's the shooting gallery on top of 23rd Street. Hepatitis Heights. Home to the luckless and the dreary and the death-sentence kids with the Virus.

A skinny kid with sheared chestnut hair and poorly drawn prison tattoos on his neck is standing in front of me, mixing up a hit of speed in a large Ziploc bag. We are in the middle of the hallway. Wormy infections blister his lips, and he jerks intermittently with the nerve damage of every speed freak who deals here. I combat the lethargy from all the heroin I inject by shooting speed and cocaine. Then, to counteract the racing effects of the speed and cocaine, I shoot more heroin. It is a vicious cycle. My blood flows like a chunky, meaty gravy.

He asks for my needle, and I hand it to him. I'm standing. I'm breathing. But I am not alive. I don't know this guy. I may've seen him before, but I can't be sure. I have so many chemicals pumping through my body right now that my senses have gone beyond what boundaries can contain, blurring the lines of perception. I feel like I am watching the highlight reel of someone else's life, its cinematography punctuated with regret, soundtrack jumbled in German.

Beyond the front door, a car makes its slow-motion way up 23rd Street, going into the projects, around the corner at the top of the hill. I hear the far-off whirl of ambulance sirens as a helicopter drills its high beams on us. No, it's not a helicopter. It's a spaceship, followed by the sounds of cattle sucked up by tractor beams. Or maybe it's only the garbage being picked up at someone else's house and a streetlight. Someone tries to clear a plugged nose three doors down, and I blink hard. My legs feel as though I am treading Jell-O. Out the cracked window to my right, into the night, next to the broom, which is only the handle and no broom, the sky is a bruised eggplant, and to my left, the door to a room, padlocked and chained, with claw marks at the bottom and around the edges, at the top and to the sides. I hear cats in heat, the sounds of angry fucking coming from inside. My bones feel congested, but I am weightless. My mouth tastes like cocoa powder and silver oxide; it smells like snow. The whistle of a train approaching grows closer, slightly softer, now closer, louder. It is not a train. It is my lungs.

I have fallen asleep standing up, nodded out. I have been awake for so many days that my body is overriding my poor decisions and keeps shutting down—but only for a few seconds—until I am startled awake by the little lightning storms flashing in my head.

Techno music pumps out of the room I used to share with my wife but is now occupied by a big-boned, surly lesbian meth dealer, whose name is the same as my wife's, minus one very important letter. I am entrenched in a sea of ruptured garbage bags. Mice squeak, frittering at my feet. The unmistakable stench of human waste wafts under my nose, and I know that I am home.

I need more speed. I am getting more speed. That is what I am doing.

There is a skinny kid standing in front of me with an outstretched hand. I *know* this kid. I have seen him before. He has those God-awful tattoos on his neck. What's his name? What is he doing in my hallway? Where is my wife? He lives by the 101 on-ramp, under the bridge. *She's gone. She is not coming back this time.* He is friends with that guy with the one arm. What's his name? One-Arm

Charlie? Bobby One-Mitt? Sailor Mick? No, Sailor Mick was my roommate who thinks I owe him $57,000. This kid has both arms. What does he want from me? *He doesn't want anything—he is giving you something. A needle.* It is my needle. That's right; he's giving me a hit. My mouth is cotton dry.

The kid has begun to tie off. I listen to my own breathing, which sounds like it is coming from somewhere far away and underwater, then it's as if someone has hit the play button, and everyone, everything returns to normal speed and sound, but I can't quite catch up. My thoughts and movement, my reactions are not quite in sync. I am searching for a vein, detached, sad, lonely. I shouldn't be fixing. I have a question.

I have to ask this kid a question before I can fix. I am sure of it.

Stop what you're doing and ask the question!

"Hey," I say, stopping my needle just before it pierces the skin of a small popped vein in my right hand.

The skinny kid with the bad tattoos looks up, rubber tourniquet tied around biceps, but he doesn't stop poking his arm, which turns poked-spot white. His nose is dripping, and, though he is looking right at me, only a foot away, he can't quite find my eyes to make direct contact.

"Did you mix this up with a clean needle?" I ask.

"Huh?"

"This hit I'm about to do. Did you mix it up with a clean needle?"

"You don't have HIV?"

"No," I say, "I don't," handing him back the needle.

I wake in the middle of the night at Hepatitis Heights. This place has gotten too crazy even for me, which is why I generally stay away, preferring to sleep with Amy in the car or on park benches when we can't get the money for a hotel room. I'd rather take my chances outside. The sheriffs should be coming any day to evict everyone. The old tenants were bad; these people are worse. Hardened thugs, murderers, hardcore mutherfuckers who won't think twice about slitting your throat for a pack of cigarettes. I watched a dealer nearly beaten to death the other day. They said the man doing the beating, an ex-convict built like a truck they call Sully, has HIV. With each thundering crash on his hapless victim's face, his knuckles cracked open, bloodied over. No one could make him stop. He stopped when he was ready to.

I have not seen Amy for a few days. She'll be back. Her car is outside. We kicked down some dope for a couple junkies to jerry-rig the alternator back together and got the thing running. It limped up the hill, but is currently locked. She has the keys, which is why I am sleeping in the bathtub tonight, next to the toilet that doesn't flush and is overflowing with the loose stools and piss of I-don't-know-how-many people.

I am not sure how I fell asleep in the first place, because the last thing I remember is getting more speed. Now I remember. I had a hard time getting my hit. My jugular has run dry. I had to use my right hand, a tiny vein buried among the knotted ligaments and tendons. I missed most of it.

I look down at my right hand. It is twice as big as my left and resembles a giant inflatable Mickey Mouse's glove.

Sitting in the waiting room at San Francisco General, which is only a couple blocks down the street from Hepatitis Heights, which is convenient since they have a working toilet and callback payphone, I look at my hand again and swear it is growing.

At Hepatitis Heights, it hadn't even hurt. Here at the hospital, my hand is throbbing and has turned a funny color, a blood red bird engorged with pomegranate nectar.

I don't have insurance. I am obviously a junkie. No one in the Emergency Room is in any hurry to help me. I wait with all the other derelicts nodding beneath newspapers and watch as my cartoon balloon hand inflates.

When I go back to the nurses' station and show them my hand again, they gasp and call the doctor immediately, and I know I am in trouble.

My right hand is so red now, it is almost purple, and has swollen to three, four times the size of my left. I am losing control of its movement; it flops around, like a fish dying on a deck. The parts where I do have sensation remind me of being a kid, back when we used to play pick-up football games in the frozen Connecticut winter, how I'd come home all banged up, extremities numb, and sit in front of the crackling fire until the feeling returned, and my hands and feet would slowly tingle hot and prickly, as though someone were sticking in the tips of a thousand sewing needles while simultaneously giving me an Indian burn.

It is such an unbelievable sight, this hand of mine. If I had seen this depiction in a horror movie, I would've mocked it as the gross exaggeration of hack writers and cheesy, B slasher flicks.

I've missed shots of speed before. This is more than a missed shot of speed. I am worried. I can feel the poison coursing through my body, overtaking weakened cells, working through the tainted bloodstream of dying tissues, easily winning the fight against an inferior, overmatched opponent.

When the doctor tells me that they are going to have to amputate my hand, I believe him. I can tell the difference between a doctor merely trying to put a scare into a junkie and real danger. I am going to lose my right hand.

They've been trying to inject a highly concentrated antibiotic intravenously, but they can't find any veins. Don't have any left. Which is why I missed my hit in the first place. Nurse after nurse has tried and failed. Without a vein to put the IV in, the doctors now must find another way to stop the toxins from seizing up my organs and killing me.

You've got to draw the line somewhere. I will not have my hand cut off. Can you imagine what the rest of my life would be like? How many times can you answer the same question? "Hey, Jacky One-Hand! How's it hanging? Yeah, man, we're all meeting up at the soup kitchen. Party at the shelter tonight! Should be a blast. By the way, how'd you lose your hand again?"

Before I spend the remainder of my days walking around like Captain Fucking Hook, I will go into the woods past the freeway, lie down, let the infection take over my body, and die.

The surgeons scrub in their paper masks. The nurses gather scalpels and forceps, pins and screws and clamps, rubber tubing and a hot iron to cauterize my amputated stump, lining each on polished metal trays, the big overhead floodlights shining down. I see the industrial circular saw, which doesn't look all that different from the kind I remember in shop class, gleaming beneath the bright fluorescents, plugged in, charged, and ready to go.

As the surgical team preps to cut off my hand, I prep to make a run for it.

That's when a little Chinese intern, a grad student from State, asks to take a crack at the IV. He draws blood in my forearm. Just like that. A small vein below my elbow. Vial inserted. Medicine injected. Almost instantly, my hand begins to shrink, colors softening. I feel the toxins retreat. The surgeons put away the hatchet.

"Speed is tricky," the doctor tells me later as he is writing out a prescription. "You never know what you're getting."

"Can you tell me what was in the stuff I shot?" I ask.

The doctor wrinkles his mouth, thinks about it hard.

"No," he finally says and walks away.

■

I'm downstairs at Transvestite Henry's. I will not go back upstairs to Hepatitis Heights ever again, not after what I've seen lately. It's worse than a prison movie up there, the way this latest influx of convicts routinely beat up the weak, steal from the helpless, force their will upon others. Watching these bastards with the Virus climb on top of passed out junkie girls, pulling their pants down and forcing their way inside, has turned my world a sicker shade of hell.

Transvestite Henry is an ugly old man. Pushing seventy, he makes for an ugly old woman. He likes to talk about books and is OK company. I'm pretty sure he has a crush on me, but he never tries anything. Let him crush all he wants, as long as he lets me sleep on his couch and use his telephone. It is raining and cold outside tonight. Transvestite Henry says that he used to be a lawyer before he found speed. People say a lot of things.

Down here may be better than upstairs but it isn't exactly high-class. You can still tell it's a drug addict's apartment. Forks stick out of abandoned tin cans. Big grapefruit juice jugs are filled with piss. Which is pretty weird, since the toilet down here works. Women's clothes are draped over lamps and radiators, panty hose, bras, threadbare slips and silk panties stretched out by heavy ball sacs. There are mice here, too, more mice than upstairs at the Heights, even. In fact, there are so many mice that Transvestite Henry keeps a BB gun and encourages guests to shoot them. The gun, a weak air-pump rifle, doesn't generate enough power to penetrate the mice's skin, and the pellets bounce off, but it still does the trick. The mice are so startled when you shoot them that their tiny hearts seize up and they die anyway.

While Transvestite Henry has been getting dolled up in the bathroom, rouging his withered old skin and painting his thin lizard lips, I've been shooting mice. I'm a good shot. More than a dozen filthy vermin are sprawled across the living room floor, bloated bellies up, claws frozen in rigor mortis, the trail of dead on a bloodless battlefield.

I set the gun down and head to the kitchen to look for some matches. I have a little dope left and want to get high. The lighting down here is weak; speed freaks hate the light. Afghans cover the windows, and only a few dim bulbs blaze beneath heavily hooded lamps. The basement smells like pungent, damp earth.

I find some matches on top of the refrigerator, which is butted against a darkened back corner and humming louder than a Vegas ice machine. Dragging a chair and using the top of the fridge for a table, I unwrap my heroin from its cellophane. Black tar heroin looks similar to hash, a pressed clump of wet, dark brown. I tear off a piece, drop it in the spoon, and draw up a hit.

When you're a junkie, it's a good idea to save some dope for the morning. It is late, and I will not be able to score again tonight. But that last hit didn't quite do it for me and I am bored, so I dump what's left of my black tar into the spoon. When I light the next match, I see that I've been sloppy. Crumbs of black tar are littered everywhere. I collect these stray bits, add them to the mix, and inject another shot.

That one had some kick. I am starting to feel almost high. I wish I had more dope, so I light another match. Wishful thinking counts for something. Black balls the size of a BB pellets are peppered atop the refrigerator. I hungrily scoop them up, melt them down, and inject them, too.

I am very high now and want to get higher. Through the orange burn of sulfur flame, I am amazed at how much heroin I've spilled on top of the refrigerator. It's like my dope is multiplying, spreading outwardly, endlessly.

This is turning into the best night I've had in a long time.

I am sweeping more heroin into my spoon when I see the first set of beady, red eyes staring back at me from out of the darkness. And then the second. Then the third pair, the fourth, and so on. Now I see all the mice clearly, huddled in the back corner on top of the refrigerator, crawling over one another, squinty gazes, ratty buck teeth. I don't know how I didn't hear their squeaking, which has grown louder.

I look down at my spoon, at all the mouse shit I haven't yet shot into my body, and fight the urge to retch.

I hit the street in search of Amy's car. I need to find food or at least some sugar. It is the middle of the night. Amy is in jail. She skipped her court date for the Safeway arrest, and they picked her up during sweeps week, which is what the cops call their end-of-the-month patrol to corral all the lowlifes with warrants out, scanning the registry at the dumpy hotels along Sixth Street and beyond. When I get to the car, I find Pinkle in the back.

This happens a lot since I broke the locks. I'll come out of some flophouse or the Heights, and one of my homeless friends will be sleeping in the back. Pinkle isn't sleeping, though. He's tweaking on speed, cutting up magazines under a penlight, like a kidnapper pasting ransom demands, a mad scientist piecing together the keys to the cosmos.

I ask Pinkle if he has any needles on him. I won't drive with needles. He swears he doesn't.

Inside the 7-Eleven, Pinkle stalks the aisles, wheezing with asthma, which draws the attention of the clerk, since it is just the three of us in here. Watching Pinkle move is quite a sight. With those metal rods stretching his neck and atrophied muscles pinning his gimpy arm to his chest, he shuffles along like a retarded runt Tyrannosaurus. I look like shit; I know that. I am underweight, and the opiates have drained most of the blood from my face. I probably haven't showered in a while and my clothes are filthy, but I am still a handsome man if you can look past the picking and skin eruptions, and that counts for something. Besides, next to Pinkle, anybody looks good.

While I am filling a Big Gulp and contemplating stealing a Twinkie, two cops walk in. I hear one of them say the word "tweaked" and know we are fucked.

After we pay, we walk out to find the cops searching the back of the car. They don't need warrants for people like us. When Pinkle was arrested a few months ago, they brought him into a back room. There was a football helmet on the floor. When Pinkle asked what it was for, the cops told him to shut up and put it on. He put it on, and they beat the shit out of him with billy clubs.

The cops tell us to put our hands on the car. They ask me if there are any needles inside. I say no. One of the cops says if he pricks his finger on one of our diseased needles, he is bashing our skulls in. I tell them there are no needles. They search the car and find Pinkle's needles. I am livid. Not at the cops. I am used to this. I am furious at Pinkle for lying to me.

The bigger of the two strides in front of me. Hand on his gun, he asks whose car this is. I say it's mine, I mean my girlfriend's. He tells me to put my hands behind my back.

I am starting to, when his partner comes up and grabs me, spins me around, jabs a mean finger into my chest.

"What the fuck is wrong with you, kid?" he says. "Don't you know you catch HIV from this shit?"

I know that. I get tested at the free clinic, a lot. Scares the hell out of me every time. But I do it, faithfully, anxiously awaiting the results and its possible walking death sentence.

"I don't have HIV," I tell him.

"Yeah?" he says. "How the fuck do you know?"

"I was just tested."

"When?"

"Last week," I say.

And I was. I got the results from the Haight-Ashbury Clinic yesterday.

"And?"

"Negative."

The cop takes his finger out of my chest and looks me hard in the eyes. He looks long past uncomfortable, before finally dropping his hands.

"Good," he says. "That's good."

12.
Leaving the City

They towed Amy's car.

The year is winding down in a bad way. We are getting hassled by the cops more, eating at soup kitchens more, sleeping in parks and shelters more. There used to be a few places in this city where I could kick down some dope and at least have a floor to crash on for the night. But everyone is gone. Gluehead has moved out of his shack and is living far away in Pacifica with his dealer ex-girlfriend, his trailer sold. Sanger won't talk to me since I switched over to heroin. I've been 86'd from the music studio off 3rd Street and Hepatitis Heights closed down for good when sheriffs finally showed up with that eviction notice everyone knew was coming. Everybody else—Junkie Jason, Ray, Tom Pitts, Leif Irish—has disappeared, either dead or in prison, I figure.

Sleeping in a car sucks, but it's better than sleeping under a bridge.

Christmas of 2000, Amy and I come up with money for a room at the Casa Loma Hotel and get off the streets for a few. I am grateful I am not homeless for the holidays.

The hotel is in the Western Addition, and the closest we can get our new dealer, Paco, to come is seven blocks away. Walking seven blocks when you're dopesick might as well be running a marathon. Paco is our new dealer because we have burned all the others. And since we continually press him for fronts, essentially a dope loan, Paco isn't too fond of us, either.

Pinkle has produced a dental receipt and pried some of his own money away from the executor and is staying down the hall. Producing receipts for legitimate items is the only way for Pinkle to get his money, and because dentistry is so expensive, he's decided dental bills are his best bet. Pinkle's teeth are mossy green and falling out, even though he supposedly gets work done on them constantly. Pinkle is sharing his room with a rotund southern belle named Janelle, who is from the Carolinas and sells clothes she plucks from the trash. She is polite as a fat Georgia Peach when she is high, but ornery as a Muskogee skunk when she's not.

On Christmas Day, Pinkle can get no money for his teeth, Janelle can sell no clothes, my mother won't Western Union me any cash, and Amy is useless outside of bed. I am forced to sit in Paco's car and refuse to get out until he gives me a front. Paco gets very mad and makes like he's reaching for a gun. I apologize but stand my ground. It is all I can do. Paco gives me the dope, one lousy half gram to split with Amy that barely does the trick. Pinkle and Janelle argue over the cotton. I miss most of my shot anyway, and my leg swells.

The rest of Christmas is horrible. Amy and I fight all day. Before he vanished, Tom Pitts told me he caught her blowing this other junkie, Vinny Two Flats, while I was in jail. Vinny Two Flats was Ralphie and Wanda's roommate, before they got picked up. It has been a sore spot since. Ralphie and Wanda got picked up because Amy ratted them out to the cops when she was collared that last time. They are out on bail, which means I have a hit on my head, dopers looking to collect a free bag if they beat the shit out of me.

Fucking Amy. Every junkie knows: You never tell the cops anything.

As night falls, Amy pisses me off so much, I punch the wall, and the nosy bitch next door brings her big Italian boyfriend to our door to see if I'm beating my girlfriend. Thankfully, Amy tells them I'm not.

There is another reason for us to be stressed. Amy and I have been sentenced for the Safeway arrest. Come the New Year, she and I will have to put on orange jumpsuits and sweep the side of the road for five months. If we do, a felony becomes a misdemeanor, and we avoid prison time. On the surface, it looks like a good deal, but it's a trap. I am too strung out to show up at 7 a.m. every day to clean anything. The authorities know this. They won't have to hunt me down. I will fuck up again. And when I do, they will be waiting.

I am falling apart, literally. Due to all the chemicals I inject, my skin never fully achieves a solidified state. I stand in front of a mirror for hours picking at my face, then wander around the city, waiting for money to magically appear, stopping occasionally to pick up a stray piece of candy or rotten fruit. I dig in garbage cans and dumpsters, and then, without washing my hands, dig with dirty fingernails into the holes in my head. Cuts never heal, my skin crusted orange with impetigo.

If I stay here, my next stop is under the bridge, permanently. That is, until they pick me up and take me to prison.

I need to get out of San Francisco.

And I know where I will go.

A few weeks ago, Cathy came up from Los Angeles. She said it was to visit friends, but I think it was mostly to see me. I have never given up on my wife. I don't think she has ever given up on me. I don't know how she got a hold of me. Maybe I called her. She's been down there for more than a year since getting out of that long-term treatment program in Hollywood. Her parents spare no expense trying to get her better, and the best doctors are in Southern California.

Cathy and I made plans to meet downtown late in the day. I don't know what I said to Amy. She might've still been in jail.

I stole a Twix candy bar from the Walgreen's on 5th, slipping it up my sleeve like a magician, and waited outside the Montgomery BART Station. The workday over, I watched all the ordinary people with their ordinary concerns pass me by, toting their briefcases and folded newspapers, sipping on Starbucks as they headed back to loving families, somewhere warm and far from here.

I spotted her coming up the escalator, from across the street. She wore a fluffy, white coat. My wife looked fabulous.

Making my way through the settling dusk, between the bright yellow taxis and long buses of the evening commute, the throng of tourists and holiday shoppers swarming outside stores with colorful bags and excitable children, I found her. She stood beneath the plaza's lit-up Christmas tree. She looked so angelic, and it hit me hard. History is laden with hard-luck love stories, I know. My being such a fuck-up and her being so goddamned crazy, I guess that doomed us from the start.

Later that night, Cathy said she was willing to give it another shot. I might've told her that I was looking at prison unless I got out of the city. Either way, she said I could come stay with her. She seemed more lucid than in any time I'd known her. I don't know what she saw when she looked at me that night, but it couldn't have been what I'd been seeing in the mirror lately.

I use the Christmas Day fight with Amy as an opportunity to break things off. The first week of January 2001, I run around San Francisco, cashing out everyone I know. I get big fronts, maximize every possible loan, steal whatever I get my hands on. I have no intention of repaying any of them. I am never coming back to this place. I know that if

I ever do and they find me, they'll beat me senseless or worse.

I sell what I have to and put Amy on a Greyhound and send her back home to her family in Vermont. Then I buy a one-way ticket on the overnight bus to Los Angeles to go live with my wife in sunny Southern California.

I am going to clean up.

I am going to be a good husband.

PART TWO

Reunion Blues

13.
Minnesota, How to Score
in an Unfamiliar City, and the Farm

This wasn't my first reunion with my wife. We lived apart more than we did together. We were married in 1996, and by 1997, she was back home in Minnesota, for the most part. Her parents would jettison her off to L.A. hospitals or other regional specialists, trying to fix the damage I'd done. It didn't matter though; we always found our way back to one another. Cathy would get stabilized on her meds. She'd find some part-time work, maybe enroll in a class or two, get a little structure, and that's when I'd worm my way back into her life.

In the early spring of 1999, Cathy was living in Rochester, Minnesota, near the Mayo Clinic, where she'd recently been treated. I had left San Francisco to go back east to Connecticut, where I was again trying to get straight. This was after she and I had lived together briefly at Hepatitis Heights, back when it was a real apartment and home, but before the ATF raid, which she wouldn't be around for. The plan was for us to meet up in Minnesota after we were both clean, and then we'd get jobs and a house and live like the regular people do. Seemed simple enough. I tried rehab in CT but had gone AMA when I remembered I still had a bag of dope stashed in my things. A few days in a dry-out tank wasn't long enough to get all the opiates out of my system, and I kept using. I stayed at my mom's for a few, my habit as bad as ever, swiping her Oxycontin and forging her signature on checks when she went to work.

Soon it was time to drive out and meet my wife. I was in no condition to drive anywhere.

I started out just before midnight in my brother's Ford Ranger that he'd been trying to sell. I told Billy I'd make payments on it but knew I never would. I guess that's called stealing. That's why a junkie rips off his family first. You try that shit with other people, and they'll kick your ass and send you to jail.

I did my last hit in Pennsylvania and came down in rush hour traffic, sick as a dog, on a Friday afternoon in Chicago. Bumper to bumper, crammed in that tiny cab without a bathroom, the fucking blues on every radio station, chain-smoking cigarettes that tasted like formaldehyde.

Sometime after midnight, I arrived at her door.

Cathy was sharing a dumpy efficiency on the outskirts of town with another junkie girl she'd met at rehab named Sharon. Both were off heroin but still getting drunk every day, so I didn't see the big deal in suggesting we cop some dope. There was no hope of finding anything in a shitburg town like Rochester, so the next morning we all packed into the Ranger and made the long drive to Minneapolis.

There are three ways to score dope in an unfamiliar city: methadone clinics, check-cashing places, prostitutes. There is a fourth way involving NA meetings, but if you hit the wrong one, it is too much of a hassle. Whatever you do, you do not want to make the rookie mistake of going into the projects—they'll rip you off every time.

We were in luck, as Minneapolis has a lot of check-cashing places, and Sharon used to be a prostitute. We learned the spot to cop was Chicago and Lake Street and, due mostly to Sharon's street smarts, had no problem scoring there. We shot up in a K-mart parking lot. It was very good heroin, and everyone was happy.

This lasted for three days, until the money ran out, and that's when the trouble began.

The girls went back to hitting the bottle, and I immediately went back into withdrawal. Sharon made it clear she didn't want me there, calling me piece of shit and a bad influence on their sobriety. Cathy argued that she paid half the rent and so her husband was welcome. I couldn't say one way or the other, too busy shaking with the cold fits—they both had good points—but I thought it sweet my wife would defend me so vehemently.

One afternoon, there was a big fight, and Sharon stormed off, only to return a few hours later, drunker, more pissed off, and with the cops in tow.

Cathy and I tried sleeping in the back of the Ranger that night. The truck had a camper shell covering it but the metal flatbed was cold and hard, and since my brother had used it for his construction job, the back reeked of greasy lube and manual labor. With a few bucks between us, Cathy and I bought a bottle of cheap vodka to keep warm. I got drunk and called my mother and demanded she wire me money. I told her that I had a disease and was now stranded in Minnesota without a penny, homeless and freezing, and that she had no choice but to help me out. My mom said she was disowning me and hung up the phone.

I knew I couldn't count on Cathy to get us out of this. She was drunk constantly. My wife had never been big on 9-to-5 work, and she was far too fragile to be of any practical use now. There was no way her parents were helping. They had been paying her rent. They would not be paying it anymore. I don't think they would've even let their daughter move back home, not as long as I was anywhere in the state. No, this one was squarely on my shoulders.

There aren't a lot of job opportunities for a junkie. Labor Ready offers one of the few.

Labor Ready is a temp agency, basically a day labor pool, a derelict rent-a-center. Each morning you show up at 5 a.m. to sign up for assignments, and then you wait in line with all the other losers and lowlifes until you receive your placement for the day. The jobs are all lousy, backbreaking positions, and after the agency takes their cut, the pay with which you're left is next to nothing. But you do get paid at the end of every shift, and let's face it, if you could get a job elsewhere you wouldn't be offering your services to Labor Ready.

I got assigned to a farm.

After a couple days working on the farm, Cathy and I were able to move out of the Ranger and into the Candlelight Inn.

The Candlelight was another skid row haunt on the sleazy side of town, with roaches as big as plums and closets that stank like pickle brine and piss, but it beat sleeping on that hard, cold metal truck bed in Minnesota in the early spring.

We got a room on the second floor. As I was bringing our stuff inside, this scrappy eighteen-year-old kid who was renting a room across the hall asked if I could use a hand. He helped me lug upstairs my big green trunk, in which I stored my life, old love letters, books, drawings I'd made, third-grade science awards, Christmas cards from my dead grandmother. I'd brought it with me from my mom's condo. I don't know why I thought it would be safer with me. When the kid joked about what was inside the trunk that made it so heavy, I told him I liked to read a lot. We struck up a conversation about books and our favorite authors, and when he said he had never read *Catcher in the Rye*, I gave him my copy. He was a real sweet homespun boy, and I wondered what could be so rotten about his sweet homespun life that he would reject it in favor of a roach-infested dump like this.

Every day, I drove to the farm. It was a corn farm, and I had to wear coveralls. I worked with one other guy. His name was Keith, and he had a good sense of humor. Keith liked to play practical jokes on people, especially the dentist. One time, Keith went to the dentist and wore Billy-Bob Teeth, which are, like, these fake teeth, all brown and cruddy looking, like a hillbilly's. You can buy them at a gag shop or sometimes 7-Eleven around Halloween. When the dentist came in and told Keith to open up, Keith smiled wide. It was a pretty funny story.

Despite Keith's ripe sense of humor, it was the worst job I ever had. Every morning, there'd be some new degrading task awaiting me.

The farm had silos that needed to be cleaned daily. In a full-body slicker, with an industrial hose draped over my shoulder, I'd climb five stories, up warbling rafters, balancing on narrow beams, to blast caked-on, rotten corn from filters. Because I was so weak and skinny, the high-powered stream damn near knocked me over, blackened bits of slop flung all over my face, getting in my mouth and eyes. Before my shift one morning, a guy at Labor Ready gave me some acid. Tripping balls, I ascended the rafters and found a giant raccoon, way up on the fifth level of the silo. I don't know how it got up there. When it saw me, it reared back on its haunches, teeth and claws bared. Scared the hell out of me. Had to be five feet tall. I wasn't hallucinating. I got Keith, and he saw it, too.

Sometimes I'd have to drop into the sewers beneath the farm where the corn slime drained and, on hands and knees, with a bucket strapped around my neck and dragging a shovel in my belt loop, crawl though fifty yards of goo, down this narrow tunnel that couldn't have been any bigger than two feet by three feet, holding a flashlight in my teeth, while rats and mosquitoes skittered and buzzed and crawled all over me. At the end of the tunnel was a bigger room, filled floor to ceiling with mounds of soggy, decaying corn. You know when you drive by a farm and think you're smelling cow shit? You're not. That's wet, rotten corn. I'd shovel the slop into the bucket, strap the bucket around my neck, and crawl back out, trying not to puke. Because there was only so much I could fit into the bucket at one time, it took all day.

At the end of the day, I'd return to Labor Ready and get my voucher. The voucher was my pay, less the agency's fees. After nine hours, which was mandatory and without overtime, the voucher was something, like, $36. I'd buy some generic cigarettes, put a couple bucks in the gas tank, and fetch dinner for Cathy and me from Taco Bell. After I paid for the room, I'd have about $6 left over.

After five days, I had enough money saved for a bag of dope. I told Cathy I was working a double. She didn't care, she was so drunk every day (I don't know where she was getting the money, but unlike dope, booze stretches a buck). I drove the hour and a half to Minneapolis. I went to Chicago and Lake Street—only, I'd never been a prostitute, I didn't see any methadone clinics, and check-cashing places proved a bust.

I had to go into the projects.

Every time I made that trip, I was burned, and I'd have to make the hour and a half drive back to Rochester— back to my one-room, flea-bitten dump and my unstable, alcoholic wife, whom I loved with all my embittered junkie heart—with nothing.

It was my own damned fault. Every junkie knows: You never let the money leave your hands.

A month of this and I'd had enough. I told Cathy I was going back to San Francisco. I asked her to come with me.

Pulling away from the Candlelight Inn, my big green trunk in back, I made the mistake of looking in the rearview.

My last shift over, the Minnesota sun was setting. She just stood there, not even shielding her eyes from the glare. She didn't wave. She didn't cry. She wore no expression at all. She simply stood there and watched me leave.

I moved back to Hepatitis Heights, which by then had turned into a full-blown shooting gallery. I got my old room back. I didn't move my stuff in right away. I figured it'd be safer in the truck. I wasn't in San Francisco two months before the cops towed the Ranger. I never saw my big, green trunk again.

14.
Salvation

After Amy and I say goodbye, I stand outside the Greyhound terminal on First Street, waiting to board the midnight bus for Los Angeles. In clothes that haven't been washed in months, I smoke a cigarette and say goodbye to the city I love.

When I got to San Francisco ten years ago, I knew right away I belonged here, like a gay teenager from the Midwest who stumbles into the Castro for the first time, only to realize he is not alone, that he is not some freak of nature; my forbidden love would be confined to secret spots in the bushes no more.

I stare up at the looming, lit, downtown skyscrapers, the Transamerica Building, Grace Cathedral and Coit Tower spearing black skies beyond crooked hills, the Bay Bridge's running lights behind me like an airport landing strip, Alcatraz and the Golden Gate, the roaring Pacific leading to the Great Highway's abandoned beachheads where the Boys of Belvedere and I used to stay up all night building giant driftwood sculptures and setting them on fire at dawn, dancing like Indians, and I know nowhere I go can compare to this place, because nowhere else can offer me what this city has, standing on 22nd and Mission, two o'clock on some random Sunday afternoon, fat, orange sun splashing, the mango, melon, and papaya peddlers on rolling carts camped beneath the giant Woolworth's sign, the Mexican panadarias baking empanadas, rich, wheat breads, taquerias stewing al pastor and grilling carne asada, onions and avocado and horchata, greasy spoons carved into alley walls and indie beaneries brewing pungent coffees, the bead and trinket stores with their Jesus and Mary candles for 99 cents, the outlandish drag queen fashions in the Foxy Lady display window, the roadside prophets promising a Second Coming through handheld, battery-powered amplifiers like two turntables and a microphone, the drunken hombres spilling out of barrio bars, whistling, staggering, sexually harassing, rough boys shouting, pretty girls giggling, Mariachis marching up and down the boulevard with their banged-up trumpets and old guitars, singing songs in a language I still do not fully understand, the swirl of bus exhaust fumes, a soft salt breeze blowing in from black waters, the subterranean rumbling of the BART, an assault on the senses, and this is where I would always be.

Yeah, it has turned to shit, and I have fucked everything up, and now I am being asked to leave, but I don't blame San Francisco.

I arrive in Los Angeles at 5 a.m., lugging a tattered, maroon backpack that holds my world and flag a taxi to take me to Echo Park, where Cathy now lives. Although we are south, it feels colder than the Bay.

Unlike SF, which is just seven square miles, compacted and enclosed, L.A. is all spread out, with seemingly no end. It is overwhelming and not at all like on TV. I see no giant donuts, no Chinese Theaters, no Towering Records on any Sunset Strip. There are no surfer dudes. This doesn't feel laid back at all. I can't get a sense of where I am, districts and neighborhoods fusing into one, long, rundown strip mall. There are more bums and all-night laundromats, and the hoodlums patrolling the streets look meaner here than they do back home. Helicopters scour the pre-dawn sky, sweeping bright beams over rooftops and trees, swooping low like crop dusters to light up apartment stoops and the backseats of cars. I ask the driver what they are doing. He says they are looking for criminals.

"That's how they do it here," the cab driver says through his three-inch-thick Plexiglas.

Cathy lives in a little cottage behind a duplex on a side street lined with tiny orange trees, in-between a used hubcap shop and a bar that's already open. My wife looks lovely when she answers the door, her long, black hair falling over white shoulders and parted terrycloth bathrobe. I ask her for money to pay the driver.

Inside, she puts on coffee, smiles warmly and says nice things. We talk as the sun comes up. Back on her medication, Cathy has a real job now, a regular 9-to-5, working in the Fashion District for a company that designs T-shirts. "It is a creative outlet," she says, which makes her happy. Sober, she regularly attends meetings, and even has a sponsor. Her eyes are brighter than I recall. I'm not sure I see a place for me in them anymore.

Cathy says that before we can even talk about being together, I need to get help.

I am a lot of things, and I know very few of them are good. I don't want to live like this, I tell her. I will get better.

My wife and her sponsor drop me off at the Salvation Army the next afternoon.

I have been in a lot of rehabs. There have been good ones. There have been bad ones. None have been worse than the Salvation Army.

The Salvation Army is not coed, and they do not give you any medication to ease the discomfort of the kick. They believe that if drugs have been the problem, two wrongs do not make a right. Maybe not, but methadone certainly helps. At the Salvation Army, they also believe the devil will find work for idle hands. So kicking dope or not, you are going to attend religious services, and you are going to work.

When I get there, I am searched for contraband, given a toothbrush, and shown to my room. It is a shared room, the size of a small college dormitory, with two beds, one lamp, and nothing on the walls. My roommate, a teenager who calls himself Li'l Stashu, claims he is a big-time L.A. rapper. He frequently grabs his genitals when he says things like, "I says, bitch, how yous 'pect me to bust a nut over dat shit?" He wears baggy pants, an extra-small tank top, and has a fuzzy mustache, the kind boys who develop quickly in the 7th grade sport. Li'l Stashu is originally from Utah and whiter than I am.

I wake early in the morning when the first pangs of withdrawal hit and spend an hour in the bathroom vomiting bile and pissing out my ass until I am left with nothing but a sore throat and tender asshole. After a breakfast of oatmeal scooped from a giant vat, I draw the assignment of "Bric-a-Brac." Li'l Stashu says this is a very good assignment, much better than "Garment," where if you don't meet your quota for the day by hanging at least 1,400 garments, you receive demerits. You can receive demerits for a lot of things at the Salvation Army: not making your bed, leaving your toothbrush in the bathroom, walking around without socks, failing to clean your plate at chow. Enough demerits and you have to work on your day off. You only get one day off a week at the Salvation Army: Sundays. Since the store and warehouse are closed on Sundays, you have to work off grounds. Currently, Li'l Stashu says they are building a new deck for the Army's director at his house in the Hollywood Hills.

Bric-a-Brac is basically unloading all the crap people donate to the Salvation Army from the backs of trailers—worn-out, stained, pink teddy bears missing an eye, chipped, cheap wedding tea sets, Big Wheels, beta VCRs, colanders, Monopoly board games, ping pong paddles, crap. I clench my ass cheeks tightly throughout my shift because I don't want to risk demerits by taking too many bathroom breaks. I'm not used to the physical exertion, and toward the end of my shift, I get lightheaded and pass out. I wake with my head half in an Easy Bake Oven. I get to my feet before anyone catches me and avoid the demerits. I need a cigarette badly but learn I've missed my last chance for the day. You get two smoke breaks at the Salvation Army, before work at 6:30 a.m. and after work at 4:30 p.m. And when you smoke, you can only do so in designated, painted squares. They do not make exceptions and frown greatly upon the habit.

Two days in, I check out. At the corner payphone, I light a cigarette and call Cathy. The cigarette tastes good, but my wife says I can't come back until I am sober. I tell her I have nowhere else to go. She says she's already spoken with her sponsor and they're in agreement; it's for my own good and essential to her recovery. I lose it. I start screaming about all the times I took care of her and what a burden she was, how she fucked up our honeymoon and killed my rock 'n' roll dreams. She hangs up.

I steal a soda from 7-Eleven and hit downtown. I am kicking hard and need a fix. I've been a junkie for a long time. I don't need Cathy. I will make something happen on my own.

But soon, I am forced to admit I cannot do that. I have no game here.

I call my mother collect, but she will not accept the charges. Without money, I can't get dope, and without getting high, I can't do the things I need to do to get out of here. And with each passing minute, my body fails me more. I slink the streets of Los Angeles, fighting the symptoms and sniffles, holding my gut like I've been knifed, resting on bus benches or in alleys, feeling as lost and alone as I ever have. It starts to get dark, and I know how cold L.A. gets this time of year when the chill desert winds blow.

I huddle in the doorway of a Korean barbeque with a potato sack wrapped around me like a common hobo on a freighter. It is the longest night of my life.

Come morning, I head for the Spring Street Shelter.

I'd passed the shelter yesterday as I roamed downtown and could tell then it wasn't anywhere I wanted to stay. Already at this early hour, the bums are lining up to try and secure their place for the night, emerging from the tents that pepper the block and beyond, little villages packed densely together like the shantytown ghettos of Johannesburg or Ghana. The homeless, wrapped in seven layers of mismatched, tattered coats, stand on bare, infected feet, raw and oozing, beside shopping carts stuffed with black trash bags and bottles. Some eat breakfast—discarded apple cores, bagel crusts, a container of mystery Chinese left atop a trash bin— as others eye their good fortune like jealous pigeons huddled around an old lady hoarding breadcrumbs in the park. Hustlers work the line, too. This is a racket for them, a place to make connections and deals, although it strikes me as the ultimate example of blood from stones. I am the only white boy here. I keep my head down and wait for the lottery to be drawn.

A lottery is often the way overcrowded shelters determine who gets a bed for the night. I soon learn that there are no actual beds inside the Spring Street Shelter, no mattress or box spring, not even the privacy of hung bed sheets. A bed here is a tiny, blue, plastic chair, like the type you might find in a kindergarten classroom. Hundreds of these chairs are placed in the middle of a large gymnasium. This is what we are waiting hours for, the prize we are hoping to win.

At two in the afternoon, the lottery is drawn, and I learn that I am one of the lucky ones.

At 5 p.m., they open the doors and a sea of vagrants floods inside. They take us to the showers, where we strip down. Rows of emaciated, naked men stand in line, shoulder blades and clavicles, hip bones unnaturally pronounced, one right behind the other, like inmates waiting for the gas baths at Auschwitz.

When my turn comes, the hot water feels so good I don't want to get out until they make me. I get redressed and go to dinner. Even those who didn't win a bed for the night are allowed to eat dinner. The line stretches out the door, around the block and back through Tent City.

The cafeteria reminds me of this past Thanksgiving when Amy, Pinkle, and I ate at a soup kitchen in the Upper Haight. We had a nice meal that day. But here, there is no turkey or stuffing, no cranberry sauce, no sweet potato pie, just overcooked noodles with salt and pepper, unbuttered white bread, and tap water that smells vaguely like fish.

When dinner is over, those who didn't win a bed are told to leave and try their luck tomorrow.

Like a lot of shelters, Spring Street is run by newly paroled ex-cons. Administrators will put these criminals in charge, thugs who have never been in charge of anything before, because they think it means their shelter will be run tight-ship and no nonsense. All it really means is you now have a bunch of crooks running your shelter.

It's like being in prison. They line us up to go the mess hall, to go to the showers, to go to the john. The little blue chairs are numbered and aligned in rows, with the ex-cons strategically stationed around the perimeter keeping guard. We are assigned a number and a chair for the night. After they take us to use the restroom, they announce "Lights out," which is misleading, because the lights in the gym never actually go out.

Lights out means we are not allowed out of our chair, for any reason. If someone gets up from his chair—maybe he needs to stretch his legs or has to take a piss—that man loses his chair and is kicked out of the shelter for the rest of the night.

At four in the morning, the ex-cons wake everyone up and have us stand outside on the sidewalk for half an hour while they sweep. That is what they say they are doing, but I do not see anyone cleaning anything. I can see they are not sweeping, because the front of the shelter is encased by long glass windows, displaying our shame in a giant goldfish bowl. There is a restroom outside, and being as sick as I am, it turns out to be a good thing.

When they let us back inside, we are allowed to sleep until six, at which time they wake us up again, feed us breakfast, whatever day-olds have been donated from the bakery, and then kick us out the door.

Shelters are for the nighttime only. The idea is that by kicking everyone out first thing in the morning, the better the chance of everyone's finding a job, which is kind of funny if you think about it, because if you were the kind of guy who could find a job, you probably wouldn't be needing to sleep in a shelter in the first place.

I find the nearest curb or stoop, anywhere I can lay my head to try to stop some of the spinning and nausea and wait and see if they let me back inside.

I must be lucky, because I win a bed almost every night I am here.

It is a bad kick. I can't walk more than a few feet without having to lie down. I continuously hack up greenish-yellow stomach juice. I feel so weak, I am pretty much helpless. It is all I can do to drag myself out of the shelter every morning and curl up in an alley. I expect to get rolled any time I am out in the street. The nighttime isn't much better, but at least I am inside, though my being the only white boy in the place, some of the brothers think it's funny to tip over my chair and laugh at me.

You don't sleep much when you're kicking—everyone who knows junk knows that—you go in and out but are never under too long or in too deep, and this time the dizziness and diarrhea are worse than usual, and knowing how helpless I am only makes me feel more pathetic. And they say I can't get out of my little, blue, plastic chair.

I bargain with God that if he'll get me out of the Spring Street Shelter, send a little scratch my way, I'll turn my sorry self around. It is the same promise I have made and gone back on a million times. And God knows a fool's wager when he hears one.

I call my father for the last time, but he won't accept the charges, either. I had promised myself that I'd never call him again, but this is how desperate the situation has become. I am going to die here. No big deal. Happens every day. They'll find a corpse gutted beneath the bridge, beaten beyond recognition, no ID, and that will be it. They'll toss the body into the freezer with all the other John Doe junkies. Perhaps someone will come looking for me. More than likely they won't. It is a depressing thought.

I've got to get out of Los Angeles.

After a week or so, as soon as the worst of the kick is over and I can move without feeling like I am going to puke up my intestines, I go find my wife. On my last leg, I arrive in Echo Park. I sit on her doorstep and wait. When Cathy gets home from work, I tell her to give me money. She says she will not give me money if I am going to use it to get high. I tell her I need money for bus fare then, and that if she won't give it to me, I will take it from her. She says she wants a divorce. I say I don't give a fuck. She gives me the money.

I head to the Greyhound Station to buy my ticket, stopping to score along the way at Spring and 5th. I cop a block from the shelter, watching that sad-sack line stretch around the corner, through Tent City and out of sight. I want to call out, "Good luck, you bastards." And I really mean it.

At the bus depot, I call Amy's parents' house in Vermont. It takes some doing, but I am finally able to convince her mother to put her on the line.

"Amy, baby," I say. "I'm headed back east. Where you want to meet?"

15.
Holidays in the Sun

After Cathy and I were married in '96, I came into some money. Not a boatload, but a decent amount, enough for us to take a honeymoon. Even drug addicts come into money once in a while. I think somebody died. It certainly wasn't from wedding presents, although I did receive a lovely set of towels and wine glasses from my stepmother.

At the time, my brother Billy was living in the Cayman Islands, working on a visa or whatever they call it there when they let you work in their country. He blew things up like our dad, employed by a quarry on Grand Cayman. My new wife and I were invited to fly out to see him.

I hadn't discovered heroin yet. Neither had my brother. It was just uppers, primarily methamphetamine. I wasn't shooting anything, either. It was just snorting and smoking. Billy did speed whenever I was around. He liked having me around.

On the surface, my brother and I couldn't have been more different. I was the musician and painter; he played football. I hung with the dirtbags from shop class; he was king of the prom. But we both grew up in the same house, and one thing we knew about our troubles: our mother wasn't to blame.

This was in the days of cassettes. Don't see much of them anymore, but they were great for smuggling drugs across the country. I could unscrew a cassette and fit a whole teenager, which is what we called a 16th of an ounce of crystal meth, inside. They sold the little screwdrivers to open up the cassettes in eyeglass repair kits.

You can Internet search before and after pictures of meth addicts, see the irrefutable devastation the drug wreaks. When you're on speed, though, you think you look fine. I'd see the looks we got from people, the incendiary hatred in their eyes. I could walk into a convenience store and have money and be ready to pay for something, but before I even asked for the cigarettes, the owner would throw me out. I didn't get it. The money might even be *in my hand*. I remember asking Gluehead once, "Why do people hate us so much? They can't possibly know we're addicts just by looking at us." Yeah, they could.

We landed on Grand Cayman. It was a small airport, and they had to roll up the stairs to let us out. Walking across the tarmac, it was hot and sunny and smelled like I always thought the tropics would, as if the entire island had been dipped in coconut tanning oil and spritzed with lime wedges. Cathy and I were waiting in the customs line when officers pulled us out and took us to separate back rooms.

When we left the States, we'd given up our apartment. We'd been evicted, technically. The Cayman Islands was an open-ended trip. I didn't have any plans for us for when we got back to the States, but that is addict living, carpe diem in action. We were homeless. I didn't think of it like that then, but that is what we were. When you don't have a home, you are homeless.

They told me to strip down, underwear, too. Bend over, grab the ankles, and cough. They had my suitcase, which housed not only my extensive collection of cassette tapes and every demo I'd ever made, but everything else I owned, too. It was all spread on a table, the tapes and the clothes, the pictures and walkman, the books and toiletries and socks and shoes, old love letters, everything. They went through it all.

I have not made many good decisions in my life. Not smuggling drugs with me into the Cayman Islands was a good one. Everywhere I contemplated stashing, they looked. They opened every cassette tape, checked between every shoe and sole. They looked in book jackets and behind picture frames, tore open the suitcase's lining, cracked the deodorant, rolled out the toothpaste. They were certain they had us. You could see the collective disappointment on their faces when they told me to clean up and get out of there.

As I was leaving, the head officer grabbed me by the arm. He asked if I knew why they took me out of line. I shook my head no.

"Because you look like shit," he said.

My brother had a two-story condo on the water. Right on the beach. You could step off his back porch, walk not twenty feet across hot, white sands and find yourself standing under a palm tree and staring over a limitless expanse of aquamarine waters and powder blue skies. It was like a Corona commercial, swaying fronds, brightly colored coral rainbows, giant sea shells and fallen coconuts scattered up and down a private beach, as ocean waves gently lapped in no particular hurry.

It isn't fair to make Cathy sound like she was nuts all the time. She wasn't. I never would've signed up for that. She had good periods, too, and when she was right, my wife was as sweet, brilliant, and beautiful as any woman I've ever met. The same thing that broke her down was what made me love her so much—a quality so tragically lonely and vulnerable, something so tender in the way she viewed the world, like how Keats or Van Gogh might've seen things. Yet, there was a definite side governed by logic, which made her less emotionally charged than a lot of her sex. In fact, that's what she used to say: "I will always be swayed by the most logical argument." Intentions mattered to Cathy. Which worked in my favor, because I didn't have a whole lot going for me besides being able to talk a good game.

I wanted to give my wife a proper honeymoon, provide the memories of a lifetime, but I brought no camera to record keepsakes; we had no itinerary, no sightseeing tours or glass-bottomed boats lined up. After the plane tickets, I was broke, and it didn't take long before I needed to get high.

My brother still had the luxury of being able to sober up for extended periods of time. He might not like it, but he could do it, which is how he had a job. In Cayman, I realized I no longer had that luxury. And neither did my wife. Six hours sober was torture for both of us. We weren't there half a day before I was pestering my brother to score some pot. I didn't even like pot, but I'd bang my head against a wall if I thought it would alter my consciousness. I only drank alcohol as a last resort. Not Cathy. My wife downed everything she could find in my brother's liquor cabinet, and when that ran dry, she walked the half-mile to the nearest bar, where they let you buy booze in take-home containers.

The guy who sold the pot could also get cocaine. I wasn't a very educated addict. I knew the basic differences between uppers and downers, the particulars that applied to me or that fit conveniently into my defense of a lifestyle, like "you can't get physically addicted to meth or coke." I did not, however, understand the effect these drugs had in terms of brain chemistry. More specifically, I did not know how severely methamphetamine and cocaine exacerbated psychological maladies like schizophrenia. A doctor once told me that there is no difference between a schizophrenic experiencing an episode and a speed freak who's been awake for three days. That doctor would've had a field day with Cathy.

After we spent the night snorting an eight ball of coke, my wife unraveled. This is what never made sense to me: how someone who was so intelligent, who was so much smarter than I, someone whose actions were supposedly governed by logic and reason and stone-cold fact, and who had gone to Berkeley on a scholarship and who'd read *In Search of Schrödinger's Cat* and actually understood the damn thing could succumb to drug clichés of seeing boogeymen and hearing voices that were not there.

While my brother was at work the next day, I tried taking Cathy snorkeling. It was beautiful weather, mid-80s, light breeze, postcard waters. I snapped on her flippers and goggles and took her by the hand. I thought if I could only provide a distraction, take the focus off her, get her out of her own head for a while, all would be fine. The water was clear and shallow. We were alone in paradise. What could go wrong?

They have something called "brain coral" in the Cayman Islands. They call it that because of its resemblance to the human brain. We went diving, and when Cathy saw the brain corral she became convinced the ocean was harvesting organs. And the giant clawless lobsters, whose extra-long feelers were magnified by the goggles, didn't help.

Walking back to my brother's, Cathy was trembling, softly sobbing. I put my arm around her and tried to console her. I told her those weren't really brains, but she wouldn't stop crying. There was a group of island kids building a sandcastle. As we passed, Cathy leaned down to them and whispered, "Please, kill me." She said it so timidly, so sincerely, it broke my heart.

That night, nothing my brother or I did could convince Cathy that her worst fears—namely, that they would be sending someone to extract her brain and put it up for sale in the Atlantic Ocean—weren't about to be realized.

I used to have romantic notions of insanity, and I have flirted with madness often. On that trip to Europe when I was nineteen, I made a pilgrimage to the home of Syd Barrett, the former lead singer and original guitarist for the band Pink Floyd, whose bouts with madness have been well documented. I used to be fascinated by the stories of Poe and that king who built those crazy castles in Germany. I read *Zen and the Art of Motorcycle Maintenance*. Such brushes used to appeal to me. How far could one go without falling off the edge? Having watched someone I loved take that trip, I found nothing appealing anymore.

My brother needed to sleep. I needed to sleep. But as soon as we'd turn off the light, Cathy would begin screaming, meek quickly turning bloodcurdling. My wife wouldn't let me near her because she believed I was in on the brain harvesting, and I couldn't leave her alone for fear she'd walk down to the waters' edge and drown the madness like Ophelia.

My brother and I emptied any remaining alcohol, which wasn't much after Cathy had ransacked the place. We thought if she just slept, she'd be all right in the morning. Over protests, I tied her to the couch.

At 5 a.m., Billy and I were awoken by pounding on the front door.

On the porch stood a plumber. In his arms, he held a grocery sack stuffed with alcohol—vodka, gin, scotch, whiskey, beer, fifths, half gallons, pints, handles.

Cathy ran past us and snatched the bag. She was stark naked. Before any of us could move, she had cracked open a bottle of vodka and was pouring it down her throat, straight.

My wife had freed herself during the night and, finding nothing to drink, had looked through the Yellow Pages. It was too late for grocery stores to deliver alcohol, so she called a 24-hour Emergency Plumber.

"What could I do?" the plumber asked. "She said it was an emergency."

I had to call my in-laws. They bought us two plane tickets, and I escorted Cathy up to Minnesota, where she was immediately placed in a long-term sanitarium. Before we caught that flight, though, I had had my in-laws wire me some money, which I said I needed to get her to the airport. My brother took us to the airport. I wired the money to Gluehead. When I returned to the Cayman Islands, there was a teenager of speed waiting for me.

I spent the rest of my honeymoon getting high with my brother. We stayed up all night, reclining on the beautiful white sands of Grand Cayman, listening to the rustling palm fronds and the soft waves slapping, talking and laughing, smoking cigarettes and being brothers, under the most brilliant starry skies you can imagine.

16.
Mustafar

When I learned that Brian Fast had slept with my wife, she had just left the mental hospital in Minnesota and taken a bus back to San Francisco. I'm pretty sure she escaped.

It had happened early on in our relationship, the infidelity, shortly after we met at Glue's shack, when Brian delivered some speed to her in Berkeley so I could stay in the city and keep rocking with my band. After I found out, Cathy and I fought, and I screamed and threw shit. When I pelted her in the head with a cigarette lighter, I wasn't so angry with her anymore. It was like being angry with a child. She was not well. It was my own fault for asking the question in the first place. Like Gluehead used to say: You never ask a question unless you are certain the answer is going to be in your favor.

I blamed Brian Fast. And for so much more than this. I blamed him for it all. It had been a while since you could say Brian and I were friends. I was addicted to heroin by this point, and with that came a new crowd. But that wasn't it. Brian had slept with Gluehead's girlfriend, too, and knew not to come around. But the Gluehead Army wasn't that thrilled with me, either. Brian had burned everyone I knew. But we all stole. That's how addicts keep going. It was more than simply the stealing. Brian Fast didn't just steal. That wasn't enough for him. Brian prided himself on his ability to get close to people, on making them care about him. When this happens between normal people, a bond forms. It's called friendship. I did a lot of sleazy things as a junkie, but I never stole from Gluehead or Tom Pitts. Brian Fast felt this bond with no one, which allowed him to do whatever the hell he wanted to anyone. Brian Fast took a sick pride in being able to hurt those closest to him.

I had put myself on the line defending Brian and had gotten burned. I had once believed in the best of Brian Fast, and he played me for a chump.

I had also become convinced he'd stolen my mother's wedding ring.

I searched for him for months. Brian would've sensed this; the Force was strong with him. He really did know things before they happened. I made phone calls, kept an eye peeled at soup kitchens and needle exchanges, took notes.

I'd read pulp detective novels since I was a kid and always wanted to be a private investigator. I asked questions. I followed leads. All trails ran cold. They said he was still in the city, but he always managed to stay a step ahead of me. But I knew I'd crack this case eventually.

On a cold and rainy night, I found Brian Fast in the basement of a crowded tweaker pad on South Van Ness Street. In the year or so since I'd seen him last, his hair had turned silver. Not white, not gray, silver. I smiled and politely excused myself.

Outside, at a construction site across the street, I found a three-foot metal pole, which I tucked into the back of my pants and hid under my shirt. When I returned, I made a show of saying how great it was to see him. I didn't let on that I intended to murder him. But like a dog sniffs out danger, Brian Fast shied away from me.

I didn't want to do it there. Too many people. I kept suggesting he and I go for a walk, talk about the old days. I even said I'd buy him an al pastor taco, his favorite. But I couldn't get him to leave with me. He stuck with the crowd and kept looking over his shoulder. A few times, I thought about dropping the whole thing, fuck it, let it go, but every time I would think that, a voice would sound in my head—a voice not my own—and it would say, *You are not going anywhere.*

I got as close as I could and swung for his head. I swung with everything I had. I was aiming to brain him, coming over the top as though chopping wood, hoping to splatter his gray matter against the wall like a Pollock. But I missed his head and the pole came crashing down instead on his hand, which was resting on a keyboard. There was the nauseating crunch of smashed bones splintering. The room fell silent. I swung again, this time striking his ribs. I kept swinging until someone pulled me off.

The pole I'd used had been sturdy metal, at least two inches thick, solid. When I threw it to the ground, it was bent in half.

That was the last time I saw Brian Fast. As time went on, I became less convinced he'd stolen my mother's wedding ring. It also could've been this fat Mexican speed dealer named R.J., a fringe player I'd sometimes score from. Didn't matter. I never felt bad about what I did. Brian Fast was guilty of so many crimes.

I'd hear, from time to time, that Brian had been spotted in the Castro or on Polk Street, hair coiffed platinum, eye shadow and rouge slathered, pushing a shopping cart. They said one of his hands looked deformed, fingers bending in crooked, unnatural directions. There were rumors that he had started sucking dick for drugs. The homosexuality wasn't surprising, really. Brian's sexuality had always been a question mark. Sometimes when you were alone with him, you'd catch him looking at you in a way that was…funny. But sucking dick for drugs was a new low. Even for Brian Fast. I once had a man pay me $200 to suck my dick. But that was different, because everyone on the street knows, if he's sucking your dick, he's the one who's gay.

17.
Rock 'n' Roll Suicide

We were recording a couple tracks at Hyde St. Studios for the soon-to-be-released CD, *Clean Living*.

Huge framed posters of Hendrix and Jefferson Airplane, Santana and the Dead lined the studio halls, the drugged-out San Francisco rock 'n' roll legends who'd come before us, psychedelic and tripped fantastic.

I'd booked a special midnight-to-eight a.m. session, which came at a discounted rate. This was fall of 1996. Or it could've been the spring. With all the drugs I took, it's hard to pinpoint. I know I had Cathy with me and that we still had our place on 23rd and Bryant, so it would've been around the time we were married, just before that trip to the Caymans and her getting locked up in a Minnesota sanitarium for a while.

We were the Wandering Jews. It wasn't a band as much as it was whoever had some drugs and a place to play. Like Paladin, I had guitar and would travel. I was pushing my rock 'n' roll dreams hard back then. I'd penned an album's worth of what I thought were my best songs yet, power pop testaments to a hard-lived life. Johnny Cash and Thunders. Americana set to a catchy backbeat with extra fuzz. Man of the people. Man on the streets. Better to burn out than fade to rust. That kind of thing. This was why I'd moved out west in the first place. *Clean Living* would be my signature moment, my shot at greatness and ticket to the bigs. After this, people would know who I was.

The record was being independently produced.

I was too fucked up to even think about playing live, nerve damage affecting my strumming, the speed screwing with my pitch.

I'd gotten Sanger to agree to play drums, even if he wasn't thrilled with my music, which was a little too earnest and Springsteen for his taste, and Gluehead had signed on to play keyboards. I had guitarists and bassists and other drummers from earlier San Francisco bands laying down tracks, as well, a total mickey mouse effort, as I scraped what I could from where.

Dan and I had broken up the Creeping Charlies, but he was still helping me put the record together. Dan was a terrific engineer. He helped write a Top 40 hit once, so he was collecting royalties, which were quickly scorched on aluminum foil.

But Dan wasn't paying for the record. Obviously, neither was I.

Big Tom was footing the bill.

I'd met Big Tom through Brian Fast a few years earlier, but only briefly, back when I had first started hanging around with Brian, and back when Big Tom still had hair. He was renting a room in the apartment Brian shared with his then-wife.

Then Big Tom disappeared. People were always coming and going with our group, and sometimes you didn't even realize they were gone until they came back. When Big Tom returned, he brought with him a backpack stuffed with $100 bills, all from 1977. Nobody knew where he'd gotten the money. There were rumors—he'd robbed a bank, a dealer, that he was heir to a swine feed fortune, had broken into the family safe, rumors. You'd think someone would've asked him where the money came from, but no one ever did. What did we care where the money came from?

Big Tom played bass. He was good, too. We weren't particularly close friends, but for whatever reason, he agreed to pay for the studio time. I think he might've been blindsided that I'd even ask. It wasn't cheap. We're talking at least 10K. It was a big backpack.

Quarter 'til midnight, while the soundmen were setting up microphones on the drums and amps, Dan and I were downstairs playing pool. It was a really nice set-up at Hyde Street, and with all its history, you couldn't help but feel like a rock star. I don't remember who was recording what that night, what particular tracks for what particular songs were being laid down. I'm pretty sure we were working on a song that I'd written for Cathy called "Welcome to Another Misunderstanding."

Tonight they rain on all these sensitive thugs.
No one's locking doors; we're taking turns shooting up.
And nobody's sorry for nothing that they done.
Nobody's laughing; it's a different kind of fun.
They're peeling kids up off the pavement.
Looking for someone's name we know in a magazine.
And no skinny art students gonna hang out here,
no token cripples drawing ordinary ships.

Welcome to another misunderstanding.
Where did everyone go?
I didn't mean to hurt anybody's feelings…

Cathy wasn't happy about being at the studio that night. She didn't speak much whenever I dragged her from the apartment out into public. She'd stick close to my side, like a shy kid might, but you could always tell when she was mad, the way her eyes would whittle icy cold, like Patty McCormack's in *The Bad Seed* after she stoned that bird. I'd been doing my best to keep her away from the speed, but she wasn't on her medication, and all my friends were scared of her. Cathy's mere presence could be unsettling. Sometimes when she caught you in that stare of hers, it felt like she was reaching inside and plucking the darkest minor chord of your soul.

I'd gone to the bathroom to do more speed, and when I came back, I was feeling OK, ready to rock. Dan racked the table. I grabbed a cue. Then I wasn't feeling OK.

I woke at 7 a.m. and they told me I'd gone out, had turned white. I still had a pulse, but it was weak; nothing they did could wake me up. They tried everything. They decided against calling an ambulance because I was still breathing.

My wife wasn't in the room, and when I asked where she was, they told me they had her locked upstairs in the TV lounge. She'd had an episode. Must've gotten her hands on some speed, which wouldn't have been tough since everybody in that studio was holding. Walking to the stairwell, I could hear her screaming, caterwauling like a stuck banshee, pounding on the walls and doors, shrieking about the imminent apocalypse we were inviting and the Freemasons who would doom us all to hell.

The session had been pre-paid. There was an hour left. I had to be a professional. I strapped on my sunburst Rickenbacker and walked into the recording studio.

I left her screaming.

Afterward, nobody volunteered to give Cathy and me a ride home. As soon as we stepped outside, we were assaulted by the light of the living. This was always the worst moment of the day, the morning, which only served to remind us we were vampires, the walking dead. The overdose had left me pretty out of it. Sidewalks melted like elongated sheets of ice cream cake left too long in the sun; buildings leaned at impossible angles before deflating like Salvador Dali paintings of melting clocks.

I was furious with Cathy. I couldn't understand how she let herself be so gullible. Near-perfect SATs, but as soon as she sniffed even a line of crystal, she started seeing ghouls and goblins. She had embarrassed me back there.

I walked ahead of her. Cathy hated walking. There had been many nights where if I'd wanted to go to Glue's shack or 3rd Street, I'd end up pushing her in a shopping cart.

I made her walk the whole fifty blocks back to our apartment.

Cathy never forgave me for abandoning her that day. She brought it up many times. But what she did not know was that I never let her out of my sight. Every time I got to a corner or went around a landing, I'd peek back to make sure she was still there. I never let myself get too far ahead or let her fall too far behind, like Holden looking out for Phoebe.

Rock 'n' roll is all attitude and sneer. Nothing beats being onstage, cigarette burning, beer warming, set list scrawled on the back of a cocktail napkin, tubes crackling with overdrive. Yet it isn't the shows I miss. Though there were plenty, some great, like the ones with my first band, Redheaded Stepchild, at The Cool Moose Café in Hartford and what's-her-name giving me head in-between sets in the men's room stall. Some were disasters, like the Creeping Charlies' gig at Brave New World, where I discovered the difference between 80 proof and 101 proof and the danger of trying to tune your own guitar.

No, what I miss are the shows no one ever saw, the songs no one ever heard, those three-day-long, middle-of-the-night, drug-fueled clusterfucks, where nothing mattered but the music. I miss my friends.

Gluehead. And Sanger. Junkie Jason and Johnny Christ, Dan Jewett, Big Tom and Leif Irish. I even miss Brian Fast.

I miss the what ifs, the what could have beens and the nights that will never be. The stories that will never be told again.

Somewhere between late night and early morning, Downtown Studios off 3rd Street, behind the train tracks, nestled in the ghetto that is Hunter's Point, San Francisco, we've been jamming nonstop for days. There is talk of a possible show in the not-too-distant future. A cookout at Thrasher magazine, somebody's wedding, a gay bar in the Tenderloin; we're going back into the studio. We don't need a reason. All our gear is out of hock. Nobody is locked up in jail. Tonight, everyone is here.

A few girls lounge around the perimeter, a stripper named Bubbles and maybe even my wife, the one I still love. Girls are always hanging around, waiting for handouts from Gluehead. We hit the Hostess truck again. Our studio is filled with Ding-Dongs and Ho-Hos.

Sanger has hauled his motorcycle up the freight elevator, stowing it next to the washtub of tools, WD-40, assorted wrenches and greasy rags. He's taken a break from behind the kit to smoke crank out of a light bulb head and tinker with the bike's exhaust.

Leif Irish has taken over backbeat.

Former Sea Hag Ricky Ryan says that everyone wants to believe there is some big reason people get high, "but it ain't like that, man, some people just like to get high." Leif Irish says, "That's so rock 'n' roll."

Leif Irish is amazing. Not as a human being, mind you. As a human being, he's somewhat deplorable, but as a drummer, he is a god. The first time I met Leif Irish, he'd been speeding in the studio for days. Decked out in terrycloth hot pants and shirtless, drenched in sweat, perched on a stool in total darkness, save for the red light from an amplifier humming white noise, Leif was pounding the drums so unbelievably fast that he was creating a vacuum of sound, "ghost" notes that you'd swear you heard but that were not actually there. It was mesmerizing.

Like a post-apocalyptic priest, Gluehead presides over his ironworks pulpit, three-tiered keyboard system stacked high, internal mechanisms splayed open, exposed wires and circuits, fuses on operating table display. Every day, Glue's hair is dyed a new fluorescent color. Today it is tangerine.

Big Tom is on bass. We call him Big Tom because he is very tall. Big Tom can be an asshole at times, but he has money. He keeps his backpack stuffed with hundred dollar bills, all from 1977, close to his side.

Tonight, we are well-medicated.

There are a lot of guitarists to choose from.

Johnny Christ has figured out the chords to a speed metal rendition of "Rocket Man." A lanky tangle of limbs, Johnny writes poetry and is the original sweet and tender hooligan.

This is before he will swing from the ceiling at the Balboa Hotel.

Junkie Jason scorches a blistering lead. He lives in another studio down the hall and was always coming around bumming smokes, so we put him to work. There is nothing he can't do with six strings and a fret board.

This is before he puts the end of a shotgun in his mouth and pulls the trigger.

I've returned from the can, untied the belt from my biceps, and grabbed somebody's Gibson. I dial in my sound. I've adopted Brian Fast's approach, all mid-range, no reverb, distortion only on special occasions. Drives Sanger nuts. Brian Fast isn't around anymore.

Tonight, we play my songs.

The four-track is rigged together with solder and duct tape. We will record this session for posterity. Dan Jewett is engineer. Unfortunately the record will be lost when Sailor Mick's crazy Indian girlfriend lights all my tapes on fire one night at Hepatitis Heights.

But it doesn't matter.

Outside these windows, other men sleep, go to jobs; they ask for days off and wait for raises and anniversary blowjobs from their wives. In a life filled with disappointment, we expect nothing, and so we cannot be let down.

You cannot fail if you do not try.

Tonight, this morning, is why we do what we do. Because sometimes the music comes together like it is right now. Effortless and hypnotizing. Leif is pounding his drums, a seductive looped groove, steadier than a metronome, a little bit trip-hop and all rock 'n' roll. With his left hand, Gluehead hammers out classic rock, Hammond melodies, while with his right he swirls the gamut of frequencies on the synthesizer. Big Tom locks in with Leif, chubby notes rolling sweet like clumps of melted sugar. Guitars crunch dirty and staccato. Junkie Jason is the best lead player I've ever known. Johnny is strutting and hooting "Ooh baby" over a funky walk down. Dan's true talent lies in his ability to decipher the subtleties of sound.

I know I have never played or sang better. I'm hitting otherworldly notes, floating high outside my body, looking down on this wreck of a man, who, for one brief moment, shines.

And this is how I will always think of San Francisco, the music and being young, how I will think of everyone, the ones who make it out and the ones who don't, the ones who get sent away and the ones who find sobriety and new lives.

This is John and Jason, who will decide that this place isn't fun anymore.

This is Gluehead, stuck for another two years in a Wisconsin prison, where he cannot smoke cigarettes, which as he tells me in a recent letter, "entirely ruins the prison experience."

This is Leif, Sanger, and Dan.

This is losing on your own terms and never growing old.

18.
The Ride Back East

You watch the washed-out deserts unfurl. Sit, stir, cramped in this too-small bus seat, forehead resting against the cool, tinted glass. There is a faint humming beneath your feet and inside your head, but you can't make out its source.

The fun is over. Because time is a fickle bitch, and she always demands you make good on any loans she extends. Equal and opposite reaction is one of the governing precepts of the universe. Everything comes with a price, you don't get something for nothing, and the time one borrows must be paid back, one way or the other.

Riding on a 3,000-mile bus ride gives you pause for serious reflection. As the cropped mountains of Colorado are softly swallowed by the broad plains of Nebraska, you get to sit back and recall that it wasn't six months ago she hiked up her skirt, pulled her panties to the side and straddled you, as you drove along this same stretch of road, fleeing a Vermont rehab, puffed up by yet another promise of golden California.

A three-day bus ride is sometimes just the companion you need to ward off the specters of time.

As the gentle hills of Iowa roll into Wisconsin's flatlands, and each mile brings me a step further away from my wife and the insanity of the last ten years, and delivers me a step closer toward, what I have to believe, will be the place that finally provides me some relief, I remember Italy and being nineteen and speeding along that train track, and the faith I had that I would someday turn into the man I knew I could be. When did the world get such a leg up to kick an arrogant asshole into submission? How did I get it all so terribly wrong?

I can wonder why I was such a lousy son and rotten big brother, and I can fret over my wife's dementia, and I can lament on the architecture of a city that I will never again see, and this Greyhound bus will hold me hostage for another two days, and I think, maybe this time, I will get it right.

PART THREE

Three Strange Days

19.
They Call Me L.A.

On the bus ride east, the other passengers nickname me L.A. I like it. It's better than most of the nicknames I've had, which have usually been bad ones I've given myself. Tweek the Wunderkid didn't stick. Detroit was stupid. And no one calls me King.

You end up talking too much on a Greyhound, sharing the personal details of a broken life better kept secret. What else is there to do on a bus but talk? You give anyone enough time, and they'll get around to saying too much. You've heard these stories before, boys chasing the girls with the stars in their eyes, husbands who can't get it right no matter how hard they try, wives who married too young just like their mamas, losers who bet the rent on the ponies, came up short, and now the vig is in. Everyone's life here is tragic, a 12-step group gone mobile.

I am having second thoughts. I get off the bus in Las Vegas and call Cathy. I promise her I'll turn it around. "We'll figure something out," I say. There are more places where I can get help. I tell her she's still my wife.

The boulevard chimes with the sounds of success, neon pinwheels blazing bright against stacks of emerald chips rising high to heaven. Stretch limos pull past and bedazzled, sequined beauties stick their blonde heads out the sunroof, giggling drunk. Sinatra croons over the loudspeakers; the skyline plays like a greatest hits package, a hint of Paris, a touch of New York and London, high fashion, the glamorous life, the cosmopolitan. I look down at my secondhand tweed jacket with the dark ironed-on patches at the elbows that Cathy purchased for me from *La Bonita y Cheapa*, and it is the nicest thing I own.

All these promises ring so hollow.

"Don't give up on me, baby. I have something good inside this old heart. I know you see it, too. It's not too late for us. Don't believe what they say. I got carried away, sure, partied too hard, but I've learned my lesson. From here on out, you're looking at a changed man, a new man, a new me. Don't forget those vows we made to each other. You and me, against the world, remember? Oh, baby, you know you're the only girl for me.

"What'd'ya think? You ready to give it another try?"

"Oh, darling," Cathy says. "We've just run out of time."

The guy I sit next to on the bus is a junkie from Wyoming. He has speedballs in a take-home methadone bottle and sells me a hit for $30. It is the last of my cash. I don't have any needles on me. He gives me one of his. I don't have any bleach on me either, but how many diseases could they possibly have in Wyoming?

As we push east, a snowstorm rages ahead of us, propelled by the Great Lakes jet stream and blanketing the entire region. By the time we make Chicago, it is blizzard conditions. The Greyhound pulls into port, and the driver tells us to collect our things and get off.

"I paid for a ticket to Hartford, Connecticut," I say indignantly at the Greyhound ticket window.

"We'll depart again when it's clear," replies the fat woman eating a ham sandwich and reading a *People* magazine.

"When's that going to be?"

"How the hell should I know? Two, three days."

"What am I supposed to do in the meantime?"

"Get a hotel," the ham sandwich says.

If I could afford two nights at a hotel in Chicago, I wouldn't have been sitting on a fucking Greyhound bus for the last two days. I don't tell the ham sandwich this.

I mull over my options. Not good. One thing's for sure: Even if I had the money for a hotel room, there is no way my supply will get me to New England.

At the depot, I hit the head and try rinsing the needle with hot water best I can, and duck into a stall. This is always a dangerous way to fix. I can't help but recall the last time I tried it. At a Nordstrom's in the North Bay, while Cathy went shopping. The police let me go that afternoon but told me never to set foot in Santa Rosa again.

I only copped a few bags of dope in L.A., which I immediately shot up in the can before the bus even departed. The ride east is long, and I needed something with more legs, so I used up most of the money on Buprenophine pills. Buprenorphine is a synthetic opiate that lasts longer than heroin. It'll keep you well, but won't get you high. As soon as the bus pulled out of port, I regretted my decision. I wanted to get high and kept hoping if I took enough Bupes, they'd do the trick. They didn't. Now I have one pill left. After this speedball, I have twenty-four hours, max, to get to Hartford, where my brother has agreed to pick me up, before I start getting sick.

On the East Coast, I know how to hustle and make a buck last. I know where to score. I have game. In Chicago, during the middle of a snowstorm, I have nothing.

"Life sucks when you only get two ten-hour shifts a day," Junkie Jason once said to me.

Ain't that the truth, brother.

Walking out of the restroom, I spot a girl from the bus. She is young, eighteen, nineteen, and coming east to meet her cousin. Or maybe it is her boyfriend. Her name is Marla. Or maybe Jane. She is cute, a wholesome college girl with a round face and brown bangs, plucky and just this side of chubby, the sort who'll be organizing her class reunion in five years and doing marketing research for the Gap. I saw the way she was looking at me. The time in the shelter did wonders for the sores and lesions, and even with my bloodless complexion and junkie threads, I still can pull off a battered Tyler Durden when I need to impress the ladies. At least I convince myself I can.

Whatever I do, it works. It is not easy to get a stranger to give you the $80 you need to catch a train.

I get a message to my brother that there has been a change of plans and for him to pick me up at the train station in Springfield, Massachusetts, and to bring what I need. Billy is there on time, and he has brought a bundle with him. This is how they sell heroin on the East Coast. A bundle is ten bags. The dope here is whitish powder, not black tar. A bundle costs $95. A brick costs $450 and contains a lot more. That amount will be important shortly.

My brother is now a full-fledged junkie, his habit starting shortly after he returned from the Cayman Islands to marry a much older woman in our hometown. I got him started on one of my trips back east. I actually tied him off and shot him up his first time. It is one more thing I have not to be proud of. Like trying to get Cathy off speed by introducing her to smack, it was done with the best of intentions. I thought I was showing my baby brother a way to combat the pain of a world that was killing him. He is in pretty deep. Soon he'll have an ex-wife, too.

We pull off the main drag and into a semi-residential cul-de-sac, where I direct Billy to park under a streetlight so I can see to fix and ask him to turn up the heat, full blast. Heat makes veins pop. My brother still works construction and drives a big truck, which idles loudly; you can smell the diesel burning. I find a soda can on the truck floor, rip off the bottom, empty five bags into my aluminum cooker. Billy hands me a needle filled with water and a lighter. The apartment complexes and houses still have their holiday decorations up, wreaths and strings of colored lights wrapped around banisters and flagpoles, smirking elves staring back at me like a prolonged accusation.

I tear off a cigarette filter with my teeth, roll a ball of cotton with dirty fingers and drop it in the water and watch it sponge the amber. It is snowing, and the shadows make it hard for me to see my neck veins in the mirror. The snow isn't falling hard, just sort of floating down, taking its time, but there's a lot of it, the big flaked, powdery kind, the pretty snow of Norman Rockwell paintings. I jam the point hard into my neck and dig through scar tissue. I know there's oil in these wells. I have to push so far I'm afraid I'll hit my spine. I draw blood.

I've come back to Connecticut plenty during the time I've been living in California, but it's usually been in the summer, sometimes in the fall or spring. Maybe I've come back in the winter, but I think it's been a while since I've been back when it was snowing. New England in the wintertime is a beautiful thing.

As Billy pulls away, I feel the rush and warm tingle of opiates. China white, it's been a while.

I unroll the window and stick my head out. The cold feels good.

Amy is staying with a friend in Burlington, some dude she went to college with or something. I could've taken the train straight there but didn't want to chance not getting high, especially after being cooped up for three days sober. I knew my brother would bring dope if I told him to. I couldn't say the same for Amy.

When I told her I was coming east, Amy left her parents' house in Rutland and caught a ride to Burlington. We've talked on the phone several times about how much we miss each other, how we can't wait to see each other and fuck. It is hard for the junkie to separate what is love for a person from what is love for the drug. Amy had been trying to clean up at her folks'. I had been trying to do the same with my wife. We were sincere in our intentions. I mean, we tried. Sort of. Now that we've each given that up, the trying to be good, which felt awful, being bad again feels wonderful.

Billy brings me to our mother's house. I know she will be sleeping. She is very sick and on a lot of painkillers, which makes her tired and go to bed early. She has learned to keep those painkillers hidden from her two junkie children.

I have some things at my mom's house that I can turn around for quick cash. I am not stealing; these things belong to me—my old coins, my old baseball cards, my old electronics and golf clubs. There are plenty of ways for me to get money in Connecticut, where it is actually easier for me to operate. In San Francisco, there are so many junkies pulling scams that the authorities are on to us. Here, in the trusting confines of my small hometown, I can scorch the earth.

I crash on the couch and have my brother pick me up before our mother notices I am there.

Then I go around selling shit.

My brother is not happy about having to take me all the way to Burlington. It is a five-hour drive from Connecticut. I make sure he is well compensated.

We shoot up the whole way, chain-smoking cigarettes, singing along loudly with the radio, laughing. It feels good, the way only blood on blood can.

It is late afternoon, a lovely, sunny day in early February as we approach the Canadian border. The skies have cleared, but it is still frigid, with temperatures in the high aughts. Billy drops me off in the middle of downtown Burlington in front of a coffee shop called Java the Hut, where two hippy kids wearing homemade knit caps play hacky sack.

As my brother U-turns for the highway, I stand there, engulfed by the throng of wool and hemp knots, the sturdy university girls in ponchos and Birkenstocks, the mossy bearded hipster boys who look like they've just come back from the Phish tour, leaning their slight bodies against the beat-up Volkswagens with the brand new ski racks on top, which sparkle in the setting Vermont sun.

I light a cigarette for these ghosts I am chasing and sift through the lies I tell myself to go on living.

Amy, baby, it was always going to be you.

20.
Just 'Cause You're Paranoid...

I haven't seen Amy in almost a month. The boy she is staying with is named Jerry. He lives with his divorced mother in a lovely two-story Cape Cod in the Burlington suburbs with bushes shaped like elephants, magnificent oak trees, and a pathway to the front door made up of polished stones, which someone has taken the time to shovel. The interior design is strictly New England colonial—maple railings and mantles, hand-stitched pillows and crocheted apples, huge oil paintings of steam-powered catchers and harpoon cannons, with a kitchen bigger than most of my apartments. Jerry's mom knows all about her son's drug habit. She says she'd rather have her son shooting his heroin in the house, with clean needles, where she at least knows it is safe, than out on those dirty streets. God bless liberal parenting.

Amy and I fix and fuck on overdrive, in spare bedrooms and closets, in bathtubs and the garage. I take her from the front, from behind, from on top, bottom, and upside down. We do perverted, unnatural things to each other. My wife is a distant memory.

I know I am dying. I can see the black edges of my life creeping in, literally see them from the corners of my eyes as they close up around me, waiting to smother me, snuff me out. And I don't care.

Amy and I have taken our experience with phony checks back east with us. Making minor amendments to Ralphie and Wanda's plan, we hit them for much less, opening accounts with fake IDs and making instant withdrawals, $100 at a time. We've been cleaning up in this town.

It is 8 p.m. on a Tuesday night. Or maybe it's Thursday. I've been here little over a week. We are still at Jerry's mom's house, upstairs in his bedroom, which looks like a ten-year-old sleeps here, with its race car bedspread and wrestling posters, video game cartridges and comic books and half-eaten bowls of Lucky Charms with the marshmallows picked out. Another girl shows up. We can call her Debra. She is looking for the same thing we are.

We can't find any heroin. We have money, but no one seems to be holding. It has snowed for the last few days, which makes it tougher. Burlington is not like San Francisco, or even Hartford for that matter. There are no houses storing the stuff in bulk. The heroin has to be shipped in from far away, like sushi to Indiana. Snowstorms clog highways; nobody has been making deliveries of late.

We have a few Oxycontins to stave off the sickness, but since the pharmaceutical industry got wise and started adding gelatin to their pills, it makes breaking down and injecting them impossible. Lemon juice and vinegar don't work, and heating the crushed pills will only turn them into a thick goop you can't draw up.

Shooting is its own addiction. There were times in San Francisco when we couldn't get anything and would sit around shooting up beer or whiskey dregs, Sprite, milk, Tang, sometimes just plain tap water, anything for a fix. Doesn't matter what you're shooting, once that needle penetrates the skin, the brain gets fooled into thinking drugs are about to be delivered, so it produces a high, the flip side of phantom pain for an amputee.

We score some cocaine because we never learn, and it doesn't take long before the paranoia sets in. Seems Debra has legal issues, a boyfriend who is a big shot dealer, an ex-gang member, or maybe it's an ex-boyfriend who's still a gang member. I don't know. But the cops are after him, or her, or somebody, and she won't shut up about it. I've been around this shit since I started doing drugs and it still drives me nuts.

Soon Debra and Jerry are at the window, and, "Look, there's a van across the street that looks suspicious!"

"Could be the DEA," Debra says.

I want to reply that the DEA has better things to do than chase four inconsequential losers around the Vermont outback, but I am the new guy and want them to like me. I'm already self-conscious about my age. After me, Amy is next oldest, but she's still in her mid-20s; the other two are babies.

Debra opens her purse. There is a lot of money in there. Debra says the DEA wants it. We have to run.

We've snuck out the back of the house and are weaving beneath the elephant bushes. It is much colder than I remember New England ever getting. Of course, we are almost in Canada. We're trying to run but the snow has a slick layer of ice on it, which makes us lose our footing, before the crust cracks and traps our feet. The cocaine was very potent, and the ringing in my ears will not stop. Debra tells us to be quiet. No one is talking. She points between two houses. There is that van again.

It is clearly not the same van, but I don't want her upset with me. I've seen how much money is in that purse. I am sticking by her side. If I can get my hands on that money, Amy and I can take a break from this bank business, which will not end well, no matter what lies I tell myself.

We make it out of the suburbs by sticking along the woods that line Burlington, following the light of the moon into a shopping center. Now we are downtown, which in Burlington isn't that impressive.

At the Holiday Inn, Debra plunks down the cash for a room.

Upstairs, we are all out of breath. Everyone lights a cigarette and inhales hard through the wheeze. We are going to hole up in this room, it is decided, until the DEA goes away or we can get some heroin.

I hate admitting how silly this all feels, especially at my age, these cloak and dagger shenanigans. Nobody gives a shit about us, and certainly not the United States Drug Enforcement Agency, which I'm guessing has bigger fish to fry. Guys my age have careers, families; they own homes and drive nice cars. They're not running through shopping plazas in the middle of the night like tweaked-out rejects from *The Breakfast Club*.

The paranoia is even getting the best of Amy. I try to calm them down. Relax, have a seat, turn on the TV. But Debra has already cracked the blinds, and sure enough, there's that van again. I say it is a different van; it is a different make, model, and color.

"They changed drivers, and they changed vans, but they're still following me!"

Debra, Jerry, and even my Amy are certain the DEA is going to break down the door any minute. I promise myself that I will never do cocaine again.

Debra and Jerry say they are leaving. Amy says she is, too.

I finally put my foot down. That's it. I am not running around bumfuck Burlington playing cops and robbers anymore. I tell Amy that when she comes to her senses, I'll be here in this nice warm room, watching TV and waiting.

They leave. I lie on the bed and reach for the remote to turn on the TV and knock it to the floor. It lands next to the purse full of money Debra has forgotten.

I count the money. There is over $1,500. That could keep Amy and me rolling for a while. I start to put the money in my pocket, and then realize the problems it would cause. Purse missing money. One guy in the room. So I just take a fifty and stuff it in my pocket. But there is so much money, all these green, crisp twenties, fifties, and hundreds staring back at me, so inviting. I am about to take another fifty when there is a knock at the door, and I am glad I at least got the fifty stashed in my pocket before Debra realized she forgot her purse. Fifty bucks is better than nothing.

I open the door. It is the DEA.

Badges are flashed, instructions given. There are five of them. They look just like they do in the movies. One of them is even wearing sunglasses despite its closing in on midnight. They all have on black windbreakers with the big block letters on back. They ask where Debra is. They've got her boyfriend; they saw her come in. No use denying it, kid. Give it to them straight if I know what's good for me.

Talk about a mindfuck. I can't even answer. Do they have any idea how much this is screwing with my head?

The DEA finds the purse. They take all the money but leave the purse.

Then they walk out and leave me there.

Everyone thinks I stole the money. Debra has big shot friends, and that money was theirs. It is not safe for me in Burlington anymore. Amy meets me at the bus depot and we use the $50 to get out of town and back down to Rutland, where we rent a room in a roadside motel. There are only a handful of banks in Rutland. We hit them all. The money goes fast.

We are running out of time.

Slate skies hang low over one-lane roads packed with mud and sludge and snow as one storm blends into the next.

We know how this scene plays out.

We pay for the night with the last of our money, shoot up everything we've got, and fuck our way through dawn until we are empty. Now it is morning. Check out time is

11 a.m. The sickness will be coming soon, and I know that despite our promises to stay together, I am losing her.

Amy fell asleep on her stomach. I sit naked on the floor and watch her, the New England light graying her skin, wishing I could stop time, find a way to place us both in a box for all eternity, because nothing good is going to be happening to either one of us for a very long time.

The clock reads 10:46. I know because I am looking at it when they come.

21.
Day One

I call 1-800-ALCOHOL from the Vermont State Police barracks. They will come pick me up and bring me into treatment down in Worcester, Massachusetts, which is pretty far away. It is an easy number to remember. I've used it before. For as jaded and cynical as I've become, I must admit that when you want to clean up, sincerely want to make a go of it, people will line up around the block to help you out and give you a second chance.

I have a warrant out in Massachusetts for my arrest. I was caught with needles and dope on one of my trips back east. It's how I woke up on my 30th birthday, naked, in a Greensboro jail. It won't be a problem if I make it to rehab because of confidentiality laws, but it could be a big deal now. All of New England is connected in the police database. When Vermont runs my name, however, no warrant shows up in their system.

I sit in a warm room, no handcuffs, being brought cups of hot coffee and cheese sandwiches by the nice receptionist at a police station where I have not been charged with any crime, as I wait for someone to pick me up and drive me three hours to rehab. Like the diseases I've been spared, the flesh-eating bacteria I've escaped, the loss of limbs I've avoided, the never having had to suck a dick for a fix, all these breaks I have been given hit home hard on this cold winter's day in Vermont.

Funny thing about that raid, they weren't even looking for us. Had nothing to do with the checks, the banks, the felonies we fled in San Francisco. They were looking for some other guy who'd rented the room the week before, some other lowlife screw-up.

I am going to walk out of here. I am thankful. No, I am grateful. I am going to make it right this time.

I detox in Worcester. Amy goes back to Briarpatch. We talk on the telephone. We say we love each other. We say we will be together. The only thing more frightening than living life sober is the thought of living life sober and alone.

Now we only have to do something ninety-nine percent of heroin addicts cannot do: get off the heroin.

I complete a weeklong detox and am let go. My mother picks me up and brings me to her house. I tell her I am committed to my recovery this time and need to borrow her car to go to an NA meeting. "God willing, mother, I will kick this awful disease."

My resolve isn't quite as strong as it was seven days ago.

Getting high for the first time in a week, I feel like a virgin getting his first blowjob. I sit in a random parking lot of a random West Hartford apartment complex, skin warming like a niacin flush without the prickly parts. How could I ever give this up? Now I just need to get Amy.

I have one thing of value left at my mother's. It is something I have managed not to sell all these years, no matter how tough times got. It is something that means everything to me, a testament to my commitment to art.

My sunburst Rickenbacker guitar, the one I used on the 1996 recording with the Wandering Jews, *Clean Living*.

I sell that guitar for $500. I will use the money for Amy and me to start our new life together.

There is a community payphone at the Briarpatch Retreat, where the program can run up to fourteen days or longer. I've been there enough to know the drill. Last time I spoke with Amy, she'd sounded fine. But now, I am having a hard time getting her on the line. Seems

I keep missing her. She is at dinner. Or in group. At an AA meeting. Then someone answers and tells me there is no one named Amy staying there. Hasn't been for a while. My stomach sinks, and I know what has happened without anyone having to tell me.

It's like meeting a girl at a party who has a boyfriend, but she screws around with you in the laundry room anyway, and then she is your girlfriend. And all it means is that for the rest of the time you're together, you'll have to look over your shoulder. At the very least, she's never going to a party by herself, and you're washing all the clothes.

I am so distraught; I don't even feel like getting high.

Amy calls a couple days later. It is early, but my mother has already left for work. Despite being diagnosed with scleroderma, my mother still gets up at 6 a.m. and goes to work every day, no matter how dark or cold. Scleroderma is a disease in which your body attacks itself, specifically the collagen under your skin. Eventually, the body hardens and you can't move, frozen in time like a statue. The disease has already taken over her hands. The Connecticut winter is bad for them and the Raynaud's. She has some cancer, too. Her fingers are often blue, the tips eaten away, ulcers digging painful holes.

Amy tells me his name is Robert. He is fifty years old, an ex-police officer and a crackhead. She is so sorry; she never intended for this to happen. I am in my mother's kitchen sobbing like a child, blubbering with snot bubbles, unable to catch my breath. This can't be happening. Please don't leave me alone in this world, baby.

I ask where she is.

"Albany," she says.

I ask her to come back. She doesn't answer.

"I will come get you," I say. "Please."

She says she is sorry.

I walk to my mother's work, which isn't far, and ask to borrow the car. Another meeting. "This one's important, Mom."

I remember being in rehab once and asking an old-timer, one of these cats who's been shooting dope since the time of laudanum and dropper heads, how much heroin it would take to guarantee a man never wake up again. He said a brick. That's fifty bags.

"A brick of heroin," he said, "will kill a horse."

"Guaranteed?"

"Guaranteed."

I phone my Hartford connection and tell him to bring me a brick. We meet in an abandoned supermarket parking lot. I purchase fifty bags of heroin and return to my mother's condo. My mother will not be home for a while.

The world is perfectly still. It is about to be over. I am not crying. I am not sad. I am happy to end this. This life has exhausted me. I have failed thoroughly at it. It has been a long time since I could say I did something right, anything good. I simply cannot try anymore.

I empty all fifty bags, which takes a while, each one sealed in individual plastic. I use a very big spoon, add very little water, and even then it doesn't all fit. It takes two very big spoons. Fifty bags of heroin gloss over like molasses. I need two needles to get it all drawn up.

I tie off and will try for my biceps. I've been muscling of late, forgoing the vein and injecting straight into the muscle, like a flu shot. To do this successfully, however, I need to hit a vein. Muscle absorbs the dope too slowly. My heart will only seize up with a direct hit. My neck is too scarred over to get both injections. I know I have a big one deep in my biceps. All the points I have are old and worn, and it hurts like hell fishing for that vein. But I need it today. I am not going out of this life shooting up in my dick.

I hit the vein. Or at least part of it. I have to work fast, get it all in and pull out, reload and find that vein again, all before I pass out.

My last conscious thought is, *I did it*. There is no molasses left. I did it.

It is over.

I feel absolutely nothing.

22.
Day Two

Angry blue ice cascades down the face of the Adirondacks, like jagged stalactites in a limestone cave, rushing waters frozen mid-sentence. The Berkshires are distant, giant bowls of soft pine and mulch enclosed by rocky crags, towering peaks and ridges, the Catskills that rise up and abort the horizon. Pick the highest point. Climb to the top. Sleep in a log cabin and name your pet wolf Sheeba. Pull pike from a hole in the ice, pack moose meat in deep freezers. Life must be simple for a mountain man.

I'm not thinking so hot. I've just woke up on the kitchen floor of my mother's condo with a needle still in my arm after attempting suicide by injecting nearly $500 worth of heroin directly into my bloodstream. I don't know how I woke up, how I am still alive. More than once it occurs to me, maybe I'm not.

The Mass Pike takes you from Connecticut to Albany via the Berkshires, depositing you in upstate New York between the Catskills and Adirondacks. I made the trip with my mom and brother many times when I was a kid to visit my aunt and cousins, who live in Schenectady, which borders Albany. The two-hour trip seemed to take forever back then. I race along that same route now.

I don't like driving through Massachusetts because of that goddamn warrant, but I have no choice. It's only a thirty-minute stretch. I'll be in and out and in New York in no time.

I can't stop thinking of her naked on top of him, doing the things we used to do, pressing her tight, young body up against his sagging, old-man parts, doing that thing with her feet and making those same squirrelly sounds when she comes. The blue icicles shimmer.

Beyond high, I am straddling the line between worlds, my head thick as over-cooked oatmeal. I am so fucked up that I don't realize I've had the car in third gear the entire time. Everything is buzzing, hissing so loudly between my ears that I don't hear the engine's grinding, don't hear its racing, clunking, sputtering. I only notice when the car stops running and black smoke pours out from beneath the hood.

I am fifteen minutes into Massachusetts.

Leaving the car with its blown engine smelling like a freshly tarred roof on the side of the Mass Pike, I take off into the woods. I don't have any idea where I am going. But I run. I run as far, as fast as I can. Like I'm fleeing an Owl Creek execution, through snowdrifts knee high, weaving beneath bramble, over dead brush, under the tree limbs that hang down conspiring to snatch me up.

Besides the tweed jacket, Cathy also bought me these tattered shoes from *La Bonita y Cheapa*. They're not so pretty, but they were very cheap, one dollar and fifty cents, and the New England winter is not treating them kindly. The sole has started to come off one of them. As I run, it flops like a crippled clown shoe.

Everything looks the same. Tightly packed white hills and trees. All these trees. Tall, short, thick evergreen gray, twisting, fat, skinny, ugly trees covered with ice and snow. The charcoal skies churn.

Still, I run. I don't stop, hypnotized by the beating of my own heart, haunted by the sound of my own breath. I look up and am delirious with vertigo. I did not wake up on that kitchen floor. This world is too grey, too cold, too fucking dead, like the nuclear fallout of a perverted fairy tale. This is where people like me go when they die.

I pass out beneath a tall oak.

There is still some light when I go under. When I wake, it is dark, black, no stars, no moon, nothing to show me the way. My feet and hands are numb. I wear no gloves. I am certain they are frostbitten. I start walking in what I hope is the direction of the car, my arms wrapped tightly around as I shiver to the point of spasm.

I don't know how long I had been running, but it was a while. I don't see any highway lights, can't see much at all. I've got to get back to the car. I don't care that it won't run or that the cops will be there. I need to get inside something warm. I can feel my breath freeze as soon as it's expelled.

I find the highway. The cops are waiting at the car. They run my name. This time, the warrant shows up. They read me my rights and cuff me. They take me to jail, where I am photographed and booked. I will spend the night here. In the morning, they will bring me before the judge.

23.
Day Three

The end is still tough to sort out. It happens so fast; it plays like a dream. The next morning, I am OR'd, or maybe they drop the charges. I don't know why they'd let me go after I didn't show up the last time. But I know I walk out of there and that my mother picks me up in a friend's car in front of the courthouse. It is just before noon. She doesn't say a word to me, won't even look at me. I am out of cigarettes and afraid to ask her to stop and get me some. She drives me straight to the bus station in Connecticut.

At the depot, she asks me where I want to go. I say back to my wife. My mother buys me a one-way ticket to L.A. Where else can I go? Someone has to take care of me.

I sit at the Greyhound Station in Hartford, waiting to board a bus back to California, uncertain if I will even make it to L.A. The bus doesn't depart for hours, which should be giving me time to think, but thinking is the last thing on my mind. Maybe I'll go back to San Francisco. Maybe I'll become a real hobo and live out my dream of hopping freighters and eating black swan stew. Maybe the earth really is flat, and I will drive off its edge.

I am so devastated that I haven't made plans for the medication I will need to make this trip. I wonder what the half-life of a brick of heroin is? I hear my name called over the loudspeaker. I know I am not entirely lucid. I wait. I hear it again. I have a telephone call.

I don't know how she could've known where I was. My mother never would've told her, but when I pick up the phone at the Greyhound ticket window, Amy is on the other line.

She is so sorry. She still loves me. She is being held against her will in Albany. She wants to leave this guy, this fifty-year-old crackhead, because it is me she wants, but he is getting violent. He won't let her leave. She is scared. Amy needs me to come save her. She whispers the address and telephone number, and then quickly hangs up.

I exchange my ticket to California for one to Albany. I have money left over and time to kill, so I score dope around the corner and shoot up in a pizza shop. I don't feel it.

I make Albany as night falls. I get off the bus and call Amy. She does not pick up. A man's voice asks me to leave a message on the answering machine. I do not leave a message. I double check the number and call again. And again. I go to the address she gave me, which is on South Pearl Street and not far from the terminal, just beyond a vacant lot strewn with dry sheets of newspaper and a three-legged ping-pong table. The crackhead lives in a tall building with more than twenty floors. The apartment number is for the seventeenth. The neighborhood is ragged with giant holes in the ground where other apartments used to stand. I ring the bell, but no one answers. The front door to the foyer is locked, so I need someone to buzz me in or for someone to come out. No one does either. I spend the next couple hours running between the closest payphone, which is at the terminal, and the apartment complex. Amy never answers.

I call information, get another number, and ring my aunt. I ask if I could stay with her for the night. She picks me up at the bus depot and brings me to her house, where I again phone Amy, this time leaving a message with my aunt's number.

My Aunt Betty lives alone. This side of the family is poor, and Betty suffers from severe depression and is heavily medicated. Though we don't see each other much, she knows what I am and does not judge me for it. Her place is small, dumpy, the kind of one-bedroom apartment that they have a lot of in Schenectady. My grandmother was an alcoholic, and when Betty and my mother were kids, they'd frequently have to drag her out of neighborhood bars. My mother tells a story about one particular Christmas when all there was in the refrigerator was a head of lettuce and some mustard. I imagine that apartment looked a lot like this one.

My aunt falls asleep. I sit in the living room, fighting to stay awake.

Amy finally calls. She is so sorry. The man wouldn't let her pick up or leave, but he has gone to get crack, and she is on her way. She will come to me this time. I give her the address. It is one in the morning. I sit in a chair and wait.

I do not sleep. I don't think I slept in jail the night before, either. I may've tried to hang myself in that cell, which is why I woke up without any clothes on, why my throat is sore. Or that could've been another time. I don't think they would've released me had I been suicidal. I am not thinking clearly. I imagine this is what madness truly feels like, what Cathy feels like most of the time.

At 6 a.m., there is a knock at the door, and I am startled from semi-slumber. My whole body tenses, heart jammed in my throat. I know that as soon as I open that door my world will be OK. There will be a pretty girl standing on the other side, and she will love me and make this hurt go away. I will breathe again. I will not have to be alone. I open the door. It is the paperboy. He says he is there to collect. I tell him my aunt is sleeping and that I have no money. He hands me a bill.

I grab the car keys from my aunt's purse and leave the bill on the counter.

It is not a far drive from Schenectady to Albany, maybe fifteen minutes. I am not on the highway for five when the police pull me over. They ask whose car this is. I tell them my aunt's. The officer believes me. Betty didn't report it stolen or anything. Cops just seem to know where I am these days, and that I am up to no good. I ask if he is arresting me. He says no, but that he can't let a junkie, which is clearly what I am, back on the road. He asks where I am headed. I tell him my girlfriend's. He tells me to get in the cruiser; he'll give me a ride. They tow my aunt's car.

The cop drops me off in a dusty parking lot and tells me to get help. I say OK, and thank him for not arresting me and extend my hand. He says I am welcome. He wishes me the best of luck, but he will not touch me.

The sun has come up. It is 7 a.m. I am in Albany, New York.

I find discarded yellow plastic from a newspaper bundle and tie it around my shoe. The plastic does not tie well and keeps coming unraveled. The bottom of my foot is bruised. I am losing my sole.

Amy answers when I ring the buzzer this time and comes downstairs. She doesn't look the same, isn't as pretty as I remember. Her skin is almost translucent, waxy and colorless. It's clear she hasn't slept in a while and is obviously high on crack, her eyes vacuous pits. I notice these coarse, black hairs jutting beneath her chin that I hadn't noticed before. I beg her to come away with me, to love me still.

But I have nowhere to take her.

I don't even have a car to take her nowhere in. I am out of my fucking mind. Every time I step into the street, I feel like I am disappearing. I have *nothing.* Amy has just finished blowing a really old man for a hit of crack. And I am on my hands and knees begging her to take me back.

I can't stop crying, a little boy hyperventilating, chest-heaving sobs, the tears clearing tiny dirt paths down my cheeks, salt and snot running into my mouth, and her eyes are so wide as she stares off into glassy space past my shoulder, like she can't hear a goddamn word I am saying, everything vacant and empty, muted, and it is that high winter sun, the kind of sun you can stare directly at and it won't hurt your eyes because it is so far away, a dull, white dot in that crisp, biting Northeastern cold, the kind of cold where every time the wind blows, it makes your eyes water and feels like pins pricking your flesh. I beg her to please love me still.

Amy says she is not coming back. I tell her I am going to get sober. She says she knows. I tell her if it is the last thing I do, I am going to get sober. Amy says she knows.

I ask her to have one last drink with me and lead her by the hand as we walk across the street to the kind of bar that is open at 7 a.m. No one notices us. I don't want a drink. I bring Amy to the back of the bar, into the darkest corner, and press against her. She tries to wriggle free, but I don't let her. I tell her to be quiet. I position her snuggly against my cock and make her get me off.

I haven't seen her since.

I walk several blocks toward the downtown skyscrapers. There is a building under construction and wrapped with scaffolding. I hop the guardrail and begin to climb. The scaffolding goes very high into the clouds. I will jump. No guesswork this time, no trying to calculate how much poison is needed to thwart tolerance. You go high enough and fall, and your body breaks. I will go high enough and fall so that my body breaks.

Bare feet wedge into metal braces, thin, quavering arms pull mightily. Twenty, thirty feet up, panting like an animal, I turn around and look down. People have stopped what they are doing. Cars sit motionless in the middle of the road. Mothers hold children's hands. Old couples twist bent bodies. Construction workers have turned off their Bobcats and do not smoke. All look up at a madman.

I think of a dinner date. With Cathy. Back when we first met, we used to go out to dinner a lot. Fancy places. I was a bum even then. She loved me, but I was a bum. She'd buy me clothes, dress me up, and take me out to a nice restaurant, and before the bill came, she'd slip me the money, under the table, to pay for it. It seemed kind of pointless. Money is money, what would a restaurant care who pays the bill? I don't know why this thought of all thoughts pops into my head, as I stand on that scaffolding, seven years later, essentially divorced, and about to fall to my death. It's just so fucking sad. I think I get it now, the way every girl dreams of her husband, this wonderful man she will marry and how in love they will be, and there was Cathy, pretending that the man she loved was taking her out to dinner.

It breaks my goddamn heart.

I remember a friend once saying that the harder he tried not to end up like his old man, the more he ended up just like him.

I've told myself that I live for art and beauty, that I've thwarted the conventional for the sake of higher principles and have endured years of torment with the belief that a big payoff would justify the misery. It is clear to me now that no such moment is coming. I am full of shit. There is nothing beautiful or the least bit artistic in my life. I am tired of fighting and failing and having to ask for cigarettes. These people I claim to despise are the same people on whom I am dependent, the same ones I beg to give me their leftovers and loose change, to let me sleep on their bathroom floor.

She was just a girl who wanted to be taken out to dinner.

I climb down, take the $47 in wadded-up bills I have left in my pocket, and I get on a Greyhound bus once more. This time I go straight to rehab. I do not pass the ghetto. I do not collect any junk.

This is the last day.

PART FOUR

Diary of a Lunatic in Rehab

24.
The Ninth Floor

A ruddy-faced man sits chomping on an egg and pork sandwich. On his tiny desk, there is a crumpled McDonald's bag slick with grease and a Styrofoam coffee cup next to a pile of powered creamer and sugar packets. He stares at a blocky computer monitor that looks like it came from the 1980s. It is morning and the end of winter. Hot air pushes through clanking overhead vents, the room choked with the ripe tang of flop sweat and cheap lime deodorant. A window has been cracked open, and cold gusts spurt in, but the claustrophobic office is still suffocating.

"Have a seat, Mr.—"

"Call me Brian."

"Says here your name is—"

"I know what my name is. I'm not that out of it."

"OK," the in-take counselor says. "Tell me, how many times does this make?"

Overweight with thinning black hair, he looks like Yankee manager Joe Torre, same droopy eyelids and ballooned Italian nose, same slow, labored movements. He doesn't wait for an answer before plugging data into the ancient computer with one hand, fingering through pages in a folder with the other.

"Total?"

"Yes," the counselor says, "total."

"Seventeen."

"Seventeen rehabs?"

"Give or take. There were some mental hospitals, too. I was committed in Minneapolis. Massachusetts. Had a 5150 in California. But, yeah, seventeen rehabs."

"Wow. That's a lot. What's that tell you?"

"That I'm a fucking idiot?"

The fat man stops typing, attempts to lean back in his chair, but the confined space doesn't allow it. He inserts a thumb into his waistline, jiggles it. His belly shimmies like a Jell-O mold. "I suppose," he says, drawing the syllables out, "that would be one way to look at it."

I can't believe I am back here again.

The counselor stabs a plump sausage finger at me. "Another way would be to say that you are determined."

We are on the ninth floor, and the view out the window is of a rundown section of North Hartford in Connecticut. I used to score a few blocks from here, over by the Greyhound Station. The hospital complex is huge, but I never knew about this place. Most of the apartments in this part of town are either boarded up or in need of serious repair—glass broken, steps missing, trampled patches of weeds on lawns that are mostly dirt, upended red plastic bicycles, little brown boys and girls playing unsupervised in the street. When most people think of Connecticut, they envision yacht clubs and private tennis courts, not this.

Out the window, a couple of nasty looking dudes in do-rags are fixing a purple muscle car below, its polished hood erect. They're shirtless, despite the chilly temperature, with prison-sculpted black bodies. Hip-hop beats pump out the back of the car, overpowering cracked, factory-issued speakers. You can hear the crackle all the way up here.

The counselor hefts a huge three-ring binder from a stack on the floor and drops it on his desk. He flips through doctors' reports and charts, Medicare guidelines, emergency contacts, the assorted personal information and embarrassing details of a screw-up's permanent record. He alternates from chart to me, slurps a sip of coffee, winces a smile.

The interior design is straight out of the '70s—broad horizontal swathes of brown and teal and mustard, natty shag carpeting, even a fake potted palm tree in a corner, the under-funded accommodations of the state-sanctioned. It feels like I have lived my whole life in brick buildings.

It has taken me three weeks and three separate facilities to get here. I detoxed for five days in Worcester, then was transferred to a mental hospital for three more before shipping off to another rehab in Boston, where I stayed while I was waitlisted for this place. I didn't have shoes when I checked into detox.

"Says here you were in pretty rough shape this last time." The counselor points to the chart. "Homeless, attempted suicide, arrested for stealing cars—"

"Can I ask you something?"

"Shoot."

"What's your name?"

"Don."

"Did you have the same problem, Don? Before you started working here, I mean."

Don the counselor places his meaty palms together, carefully lining up the fingers, the backs of which are coated with thick black fur. "Is that important?"

"I've never met anyone who's actually kicked heroin. I've met plenty of recovering alcoholics, some cokeheads, pill poppers. I've *heard* about guys who've kicked junk, just never met one."

"And what would you say if I told you that I had?"

"Then I guess I would've met one. But you don't look like a junkie to me."

"No? And what does a junkie look like?"

"No offense, Don, but they're usually not so...fat." It's a mean thing to say, and I feel bad once I say it. I want to believe it is because I am frustrated. There is no way I can spin this in my favor, not anymore. I used to feel cool, playing in rock 'n' roll bands, getting fucked up, being bad, the girls and the city. Being a junkie was being part of a rich tradition. Dee Dee Ramone. Lenny Bruce. Jim Carroll. A Johnny-Cash-middle-finger-fuck-you to the world. I was cocksure and twenty then. I am thirty-one years old now. I feel stupid. Embarrassed, humiliated and stupid.

Don peers down at his bulging gut, rubs it affectionately. "You know what they say in NA: Put down the spoon, pick up the fork." Then he narrows his eyes and leans forward, gives me a wink. "Right now, I'd say weight management is probably the least of your worries, don't you think?"

This place isn't like Briarpatch, which is just short of a Napa Valley spa. They won't let me go back there, though. The last time I was at Briarpatch, back when I left with Amy seven, eight months ago, things got ugly. They gave me a hard time about leaving with her, and I got mad and threw some chairs at the staff. It's for the best, since Briarpatch only lets you stay for a couple of weeks. I need to be locked up.

I am locked up. The ninth floor is a lockdown ward, which means I can't leave. It's not like prison because I can sign out if I want to, and after a couple days and some wrangling with doctors and administrators, they'd have to let me go as long as I am not deemed a danger to myself or others. Since I just tried committing suicide, they'd have a good case if they wanted to keep me.

"Which judge ordered you here?" a patient asks as I wait in the hallway to be handed off to the next counselor. Gangly, with an obvious homemade haircut and all gums, like a slightly more functional Pinkle, he holds a chocolate Ensure supplement drink, which is what they prescribe to emaciated addicts when they first come in off the streets to get their weight back up. It's basically concentrated nutrition in a can and tastes like cocoa-flavored chalk.

"I wasn't ordered," I say. "I came in on my own."

The guy sets down his Ensure, gives me the stink eye. He tries to wrap his brain around what I just said. "Wasn't court-ordered?" he repeats. It's like I just told him that I am not bi-pedal or don't breathe air. "What the fuck you doing here then?"

The next counselor comes out of the office. This one is short, bald, and speaks with a thick Scottish brogue. I am guessing alcoholic. He shows me to my room.

It is a shared room. My new roommate is lying on his bed reading a James Paterson book. He doesn't look up.

Scot takes me through the rules as he shows me around. Isn't much to see. Tan accents on white walls, green tiled floors, overhead fluorescent lights, couple water fountains, bathrooms with timers on the doors, stiff scents of disinfectant orange and bleach, a hospital. There are a lot of rules. Most of these have to do with respecting others' boundaries. You don't want to violate these rules.

I ask where we smoke. He brings me to the smoking room, a 10-x-20 space yellowed by time and tar, the millions of cigarettes smoked by losers just like me. The room smells like a musty cardboard box stuffed with wool sweaters that's been left in a hot attic. The view overlooks Blue Hills Avenue and the hospital's employee parking lot. There is only one other patient in the smoking room, a man with Charlie Manson eyes and straggly beard. He does not pay attention to us. His head rests against the glass as he stares blankly at the outside world. He lights a cigarette from the one he's just finished and sucks so hard, half of it instantly turns to ash.

I am taken to where we eat our meals. It is not a separate dining room, just a cordoned off square in the middle of the floor between the locked front doors and reception area, slightly larger than a decent-sized living room. There are two rows of half a dozen brown tables with blue plastic chairs around them, enclosed by half-wall partitions. Sort of like a high school cafeteria. Actually, it reminds me more of the Spring Street Shelter. There will be three meals at the same time every day. There are a lot of rules that go along with eating here.

Scot points out the payphone, which is next to the dining area. There is only one payphone on the unit. Using it is a privilege, not a right. You sign up at 6 a.m. every morning for ten-minute slots. You don't want to be late to sign-up; these spots fill up quickly.

Men and women shuffle about, slinking in and out of groups, back to their rooms to retrieve notebooks or pens, candy, cigarettes.

Judging from the rooms, the dining tables, the names I see on the E-Z Erase boards, I am guessing there might be fifty patients in here. Most of them look like I feel. Drained, down, depressed.

This is the Intensive program. It is twenty-eight days and where you come after you detox, if you qualify. Detox will only keep you for a few days, so most of these people are still in withdrawal. Hell, it's been a month for me, and I am still in withdrawal.

And this is just the beginning. I can't leave the ninth floor after twenty-eight days. I've done that enough to know it will not work. Down the hall, there is another program, a much smaller, more exclusive program. It is called Advanced. That is where you go if you are serious about getting better. The in-take counselor, Don, explained that to me. I told him that I am serious. He said everyone who comes in says they are serious. I said I don't care about them; I really am. He said at the end of twenty-eight days a lot of people change their minds.

I am taken to the med station. This is where they will give me my pills every morning. I am on a lot of pills. A few are to ease the discomfort of the kick. Most are to stabilize me. The worst of the detox may be over, at least in terms of my physical reaction, but I have been abusing my body for a long time, messing with my brain's natural chemistry, its dopamine and serotonin levels. They are trying to get those chemicals back to normal. Or as normal as they will ever be. I have been prescribed anti-psychotics, too, which is what happens when you try to kill yourself.

They need to draw my blood. The nurse wraps a tourniquet around my arm and digs with her needle inside my elbow, even though I repeatedly tell her that what she feels in there is not a vein but scar tissue. Every time I get blood taken, it's the same drill, needles piercing ligaments, tearing tendons. It hurts like hell. They never believe me and keep gouging until satisfied. They are never successful. They never apologize. The nurse finally tries my hand, where she gets a tiny one and we get almost half a vial filled before the vein blows out and my hand swells puffy.

"That'll have to do," the nurse says.

I feel bad for her. Trying to draw blood from a junkie has to be the worst job in the world.

Now I get to sweat the next two weeks waiting for the test results and their possible walking death sentence.

"That's it," Scot says, as we walk away from the nurse's office. "Take it easy the rest of the morning. After lunch, you can start your groups."

As he leaves, I see some of the Advanced patients returning to their side. They have carpeting over there and brighter lights, actual lamps instead of flickering fluorescent. I feel like a freshman spying the cool seniors driving their retooled Camaros to school. They all seem healthy, grown-up. They are better dressed, with sweaters that look like they came from actual retail stores instead of the Goodwill bargain bin, their hair cut by professionals, combed, styled. They wear nice shoes. They joke. They laugh. Their cheeks have color. They walk with a purpose. I want what they have.

25.
Doctor Stevens

Dr. Stevens is my doctor. You get assigned a doctor when you check into these places so they can prescribe you medicine and monitor your progress. I have never stayed long enough to demonstrate any real progress. Dr. Stevens doesn't seem much older than I am. But he seems a lot older than I am, if you know what I mean. He has a red beard and wears glasses, but the beard is neatly trimmed and the glasses thin-framed and hip. I've met with him several times since I've been here. I could tell right away something separates him from other doctors I've had. I can't quite put my finger on why he is different. We do the same thing I've done with other doctors. I complain, he listens, decides which meds I need. Doctors are big on history, so we start at the beginning.

We meet every day for twenty minutes in his office, where we mostly talk about my dad and Little League. We haven't gotten to the heavy stuff yet. I guess there is no hurry. I am going to be here a while.

AMA and self-help books are neatly stacked on shelves carved into a white wall behind him. There is a poster of Christopher Columbus on the back of the door. The explorer wears a flowing purple robe. He stands with one foot on the bow of a ship and a "full-steam ahead" expression. The caption reads: *If he wasn't looking, he never would've found it.*

"How are you sleeping?" Dr. Stevens asks me.

"I don't sleep much." Because of my recent history, they have me on suicide watch, which means the door to my room has to stay open all night, and the bright lights from the hallway are always on. Plus someone comes by every fifteen minutes to shine a flashlight in my face. A couple nights of this and my roommate asked to be assigned another room, which means mine is now private. Fine by me.

"We'll start you on something," Dr. Stevens says. "See if that helps. How are you feeling otherwise?"

I know he has to ask these questions, but I also know he knows the answers. Even though I haven't used in over a month and am still on methadone, without the heroin, which has been my real wife for so long, I am a wreck. Heroin takes away all pain, physical and emotional. Without the drug, these things have returned, full-bore and pissed off.

"I feel fine," I say.

"Fucked up, insecure, neurotic, and emotional," Dr. Stevens says, drolly. "Not depressed at all?"

"Yeah, I'm depressed. I mean, of course, I'm depressed. Who wouldn't be depressed?" Truth is, I have an awful case of the fuck-its. Halfway through twenty-eight days, my gung-ho determination is wavering. I don't have enough left inside me to go through this. I've been an addict for too many years. I've disappointed everyone, lost everything I ever gave a damn about. I can't even drive a car when I get out because of the Massachusetts mess. I'll be a thirty-something jackoff pedaling a fucking bicycle to get around. I feel as rotten as a man can feel, and a few blocks away is my relief. A few short blocks. Seems a hell of a lot easier walking down that path than up this one in front of me.

Dr. Stevens pulls out his pocket knife and begins cleaning his fingernails. It is not a big knife, just a little thing, but the timing seems strange given the circumstances.

"You're not thinking of leaving us?" he asks. It's not really a question.

I can't imagine that the knife is being used as intimidation, but you have to admit, the timing's weird.

"I don't know what I'm going to do," I say. "I'm tired of trying and failing, y'know? I keep doing the same thing over and over—"

"You know what the definition of insanity is?"

Yes, I say, I know: "Doing the same thing over and over again and expecting different results." Like the acronym for "fine," and Chapter Five of the Big Book, which is the Alcoholics Anonymous bible, and all the other bumper sticker slogans they cram down your throat in rehab. Easy Does It. One Day at a Time. Stinkin' Thinkin'. I've had enough of these pithy sound bites to last a lifetime.

Dr. Stevens smirks. He is slightly smug, waving that little knife, maybe even arrogant. But I feel comforted around him. Or as comforted as I can feel these days. I want to say that he is a good man. He reminds me of Morgan Freeman in that Michael Keaton movie where he's a cokehead who kills a hooker. We watched it in group this morning. A tough but caring advocate in a demanding but thankless field. Except, you know, younger. And white. I can't help but think how much Brian Fast would hate him.

"How's everything else going?" he asks.

"Like what?"

"Like your mental faculties, your thought processes."

"My memory's all fucked up."

"How so?"

"I'm confused. Lately I've been feeling, like, I don't know, maybe time isn't so linear, everything sort of overlaps, like my whole life is happening all at once. I mean, I know I was in the Cayman Islands *before* Minnesota, and I know the year I lost my job was before I met this person or that, and I know I slept with this girl *before* I met another, but it doesn't always seem that way when I think about it. It's like I was in both places at once. I don't know how else to explain it."

"I wouldn't worry about it," Dr. Stevens says. "That's not uncommon, especially with all the drugs you were taking, for as long as you were taking them. Things will straighten out." He doesn't look up when he says this, just keeps wiggling the tip of the pocket knife. "Your body and brain need to flush out all the garbage." He puts his knife down on the desk, but doesn't close it, its tiny tip extended toward me. "Have you thought about what you're going to do?"

"What do you mean?"

"With your life, when you get out of here? You're not going to be here forever."

It seems like such an obvious question, but it's caught me completely off-guard. I've been living day-to-day for so long. I haven't had to think any further ahead than my next $20, my next score, my next hotel room, my next meal.

"I don't know," I say. "I don't really like playing guitar when I'm off drugs. I like singing, but I'm not very good at it. Maybe I'll start painting again."

"I'm talking about bigger things—a direction, work, a career. Where you are going to live."

"My mom said I could stay with her." I toe the strap on my sandal. They gave me a pair of sandals from Lost and Found when I was up in Massachusetts. They were the only shoes they had. My mother has already come by here and dropped off some clothes and cigarettes, a phone card and a bunch of books, but she didn't bring me any shoes because she said she didn't know my shoe size anymore. I bounce in the chair, try to get comfortable. "I haven't really thought about it."

"Perhaps you should." Dr. Stevens picks up the pocket knife again, waggles it at me. "And one more thing."

"What?"

"I want you to start keeping a diary."

"A diary? Like girls keep?"

"Call it a journal, if it makes you feel better."

"Why?"

"I think it will help with your 'time not being linear' problem."

"OK," I say, even though I think it is a stupid idea.

26.
Group Part I

Dear Diary,

I sent Cathy flowers for her birthday. When we were married, I never bought her gifts, not for her birthday, not for Christmas or Valentine's. I wouldn't even make her a card. Now that I'm not hustling 24/7, I have time for those little things that I should've cared about before, like sending flowers to someone I love on her birthday.

I called her, and she thanked me for the flowers. She said they were beautiful. I told her I was sorry.

Chairs are stationed in a tight circle. Everyone drinks ginger ale from paper cups. It is just before noon. This is Men's Group.

William is in the middle of a story. Big and black, with a shaved head and arms like railroad ties, William Jacks could've been a heavyweight prizefighter in another life. In fact, he actually looks a little like Earnie Shavers, who was one of my father's favorite fighters after he went the full fifteen with Ali. I remember watching that fight with my dad. They beat the hell out of each other. I was seven years old. It was around the time my father threw my mother down a flight of stairs and broke her leg.

"What happened?" someone asks.

"Dude from the rental place shows up, this tall, blond geek—looks like one of them Mormon fuckers, all spiffy, jacket and tie. He says, 'Mr. Jacks, I'm from Rent-a-Center.

We've been trying to call the number you gave us, but it's out of service.' I say, 'No shit it's out of service.'"

There are a few chuckles. Sunshine beats through the long, reinforced window, across the faded gold carpet.

He goes, "'Mr. Jacks, I've come for our TV,' and I go, 'Don't got it.'"

Guys roll their eyes, shake their heads. Nobody here is dressed in hospital gowns like they are down on the sixth floor, the detox unit, or even like they are on the other side in Intensive, with their Goodwill rags, donated shoes, and sad eyes. They dress in regular clothes over here, shirts with collars and blue jeans. They even let you keep hair gel in your room on this side, despite the trace alcohol content.

"'What do you mean you don't have it?' he says. And I go, 'Just what I said, mutherfucker—*I don't got it!*'" William smiles wide. "It's like this guy's just got off the boat from Iowa."

Everyone laughs harder.

I've recently been moved to Advanced, which means I will be in the hospital another four months. I was worried they might make me leave when my twenty-eight days were up, and I knew I wasn't ready to do that yet.

An older guy who looks like the Crypt Keeper sits in the back, taking notes, but he doesn't say much. He's merely a facilitator. By the time they get here, patients are supposed to be taking a more active role in their recovery.

It can get pretty intense in group. The group this morning, the one before this group, it got pretty intense. That one, like a lot of the others, was a mixed group with Intensive patients, and everything is more desperate at that stage.

"This guy is standing in my doorway," William continues, "craning his neck to look past me, and of course the place is empty. I got a rug I hauled out the dumpster, some cardboard over the window, and that's it.

This joker still doesn't get it. So I say, 'Dude, I sold the TV. Look around you, man. I'm a drug addict. I sell everything I get my hands on for drugs. What you gonna do? Call the collection agency.' And I slam the door."

The room busts up. It's funny because we've all done the same thing, or something worse. We're members only, a secret fraternity, a depraved Moose Lodge. Normal people don't do these things, and they are rarely funny at the time. They're called "war stories" and you've got to be careful when you're telling them not to glorify the drug lifestyle. New patients do that a lot. I do that a lot.

There are a few ragged coughs before the room settles down.

It isn't as depressing over here as it is in a twenty-eight day program, which is filled with zombies, everyone gaunt, bloodless, infected. When you first come in, you're shell casing, an invisible man. They take your vitals to make sure you won't die, feed you protein shakes, sedate you and it's off to bed. I know I'm not out of danger but it finally feels like I'm moving forward, toward something better, however far away that may still be.

A big E-Z Erase board hangs on the far wall, with patients' names written in black magic marker on tape along the side, the week and month across the top, forming little squares. Inside these squares, blue, silver, and gold stars rank patients for how well they are working their recovery. I want a gold star. I know it's stupid, but I want to be acknowledged for doing something well.

"I used to go to the Spanish markets," another patient, Mark, says. Mark is older than most of these men, silver hair and slight build, a twinkle in his gray-blue eyes lending resemblance to a latter-day Paul Newman. He looks dignified. "You know how they sell Valium out of those markets?"

"Mangoes and diazepam," someone says.

"I'd ring them up. 'Hello. I'm Officer Ribald,' I'd say. 'I'm calling to see if you'd like to make a $200 donation to the Policeman's Ball.'"

Mark stops. The room waits for the punch line.

"Then what?"

"That's it," Mark says. "Next day, I put on a nice shirt and tie, go down to the market and introduce myself as Officer Ribald. 'I'm here to pick up a donation for the Policeman's Ball.' They'd hand me an envelope with two bills in it."

"Just like that?"

"Worked every time." Mark sighs, looks out the window. "Of course, you couldn't do it that often."

I wonder how many of these guys are going to make it. I read somewhere that the success rate in these places is only one out of thirty-four, and that's not factoring in the dismal junkie stats. There are only a dozen people in Advanced, men and women combined.

I do the math. Doesn't look good.

"What about the new guy," someone asks, motioning to me.

I sit up. "Don't have much to say. Came on a bus from L.A., left a wife behind, screwed everything up. I've been in Intensive for the last month, got moved over to Advanced on Friday. I want to get straight."

There are a couple muffled snickers.

"Well," someone says, "that *is* the idea, ain't it?"

27.
Recovering Junkie Girls

Dear Diary,

I got the test results back. Negative. Again. For the past ten years, I have lived in a city where 95% of the junkies are infected with either Hep C or the Virus or both. I've been careful, sure, but it doesn't mean there haven't been times where I've been stupid, too.

I have to thank my mom for getting all her church friends to pray for me. I don't believe in that stuff so much. But I don't believe I've been that lucky, either.

I've made a new best friend. His name is Daryll, with two "l"s. Unlike me, Daryll is a real bank robber.

"Holding up banks gets a bad rap," Daryll says. "The success rate is actually quite good. You get away with your first bank robbery eighty percent of the time. Problem is," he says, "you go back a second."

Daryll just got out of prison. He is older than I am and has Hep C. We hit it off immediately.

I met him in group when I told him he has nice eyes. He does, too. Never seen such a brilliant shade of blue before. They're bright cobalt, almost luminescent, with little sparkles in them. It was funny when I said it to him, because men don't usually say that sort of thing to each other. I've ended up taking a leadership role in here, so I'll say whatever the hell I want, if I'm in the mood.

That's how we spend all our time in the hospital. Group. Group in the morning. Group before lunch, and after lunch and in the afternoon and at night. Then there's AA and NA and CA and GA, and I don't even have a gambling problem, but I can see how it's all the same. This is what my life has been like for the past few months, one long therapy session, baring my soul to strangers about all the fucked-up shit I've done.

I've traveled all across America, north, east, south and west, even spent time in the tropics and overseas in Europe. I stayed a month on a Greek isle, ate exotic meat pies and slept on a crooked bed. I once remained awake for seventeen days in a row. I have a criminal record. I'd like to believe I've lived a fairly eventful life, however misguided at times. As tough as it got, it was rarely boring. Now my whole life is spent on one floor of a lockdown ward, and the funny thing is it's the best I've felt in ages.

I do well with routine. Left to my own devices, my results tend to suck.

My favorite group is Men's Group. It's raw, unguarded. Nothing is off limits. We get real. We get to curse and talk about man stuff.

We talk about women, mostly.

After Men's Group, Daryll says to me, "I think I am more addicted to the girls than I am the drugs."

I don't respond.

"Recovering junkie girls forever," Daryll says with a laugh. "I can't keep away from them. I can stop shooting the junk for a while. I can get a job, pay my bills, work the program, but I can't stay away from the girls."

He doesn't need to tell me that. Drugs and girls are the same to me: an escape, a means to get away from me, whose company I have grown sick to death of.

Addicts are plagued by drug dreams in rehab. We all get them, and you find out how similar they are, a variation on a single theme: the chase.

It's late at night, black, raining, cold, in a hopeless city or some forgotten town, you're alone, and you can feel it calling you from the lost side of forever. You're always missing something in these dreams—the money, the drug, a needle, the vein, a place to fix, something. So you are on the run. And you know you are on your own, that nobody is helping you out. Through your childhood house and the cracked-out drug dens, you keep running, because something is chasing you, too, and you can't slow down because if it catches you, it will never let you go. You fight like a drowning man to stay afloat; you fight every urge to pack it in and give up. Then you finally get your hands on whatever it is you need; you get the dope down in the spoon, get it mixed up, you're tied off, locked and loaded, about to register, about to get high, and then…"Knock, knock, time to get up!"

Tonight, I hear her voice. It is late, raining, cold. I hear her calling me from the far side of the city. I run to her. Down the farming roads of my hometown, across the cow fields and heartland, over the Golden Gate into San Francisco. Through the Mission churches, shelters, and shooting galleries, I can't stop running, because the cops are after me, the dealers I've ripped off, too, everyone I've wronged and fucked over and screwed up. I look for friends to help me, but they are nowhere to be found. Her voice comes in and out, like a left of the dial radio station that clings to its last taste of frequency in Montana, and I can feel my heart in this dream, the hollowness of its beating, the loneliness of it all, and just as I am about to give in, fall upon my knees and let them catch me, there she is standing right in front of me, and she looks just like I remember her, from that very first day, so young and pretty, and as I move closer to hold her, I can smell her hair and feel her warmth, and I'm saying, "I knew you'd come back. I knew you wouldn't leave me alone in this world, baby," and I almost have her in my arms, can almost taste her scent, and then…"Knock, knock, time to get up!"

During dinner, where we all sit like we're still in high school, one of the counselors comes to the cool table and asks me to come with him.

"We have a problem," he says. "There's a girl downstairs who appears to be under the influence. She says she's here to pick you up."

"What's her name?" I ask.

"Lily Jane," the counselor says.

Fuck. I met Lily Jane a few months ago when I was at that rehab in Boston, after Amy and Albany, after I detoxed, while I was wait-listed for this place. Lily Jane was very young. And very rich. And very married. She had a rock on her finger the size of your head and a new baby at home. We made out a couple times after group, had sex one afternoon after I was discharged. I figured it was Suffragette City, y'know?

Lily Jane had been in outpatient for a mild cocaine problem, really just a college kid saddled with too much responsibility too soon gone wild. I might not have gone after her except that the other guys kept talking about what a fox she was. She *was* good-looking, too, immaculately presented, Banana Republic leisure, that high-class type you want to fuck if only to dirty her up a bit. The Amy rejection stung but I was trying to break habits. I guess I needed the validation more. I liked the way the other guys looked at me after that.

Lily Jane and I got caught fooling around outside at the picnic tables during smoke break one day. Another patient, a woman, saw us and reported it. You can't do that sort of thing in rehab. The woman who reported it was a ragged, old hag junkie at forty. Sometimes, it happens like that.

A staff member reprimanded me, but they didn't kick me out or anything. In fact, the guy who scolded me was sort of smirking while he did it. I half expected him to break out a high-five.

That afternoon, after Lily Jane had left for the day, I was watching TV in the patient lounge when the hag junkie who'd done the ratting told me dinner was ready. She was holding a little carton of milk. I was so mad. I thought of the meanest thing I'd ever heard anyone say and hurled it back, just as calmly and viciously as Sanger had said it: "Shut up, you stupid junkie."

The hag threw her milk at me and broke down, sobbing.

The timing to get into this place wasn't perfect, and I had a couple days to kill when I was released before I could catch my bus. I called Lily Jane. I didn't know anyone else in Boston. I didn't trust myself down in the Hartford, not with my brother still running. Lily Jane picked me up at a coffee shop around the corner.

She got us a $300 a night hotel room downtown. She paid cash, so her husband wouldn't see it on the credit card bill. It was huge, swanky, way up there on the important floors. They had monogrammed robes and those creamy white soaps shaped like seashells that you secretly want to eat.

We fucked all afternoon, six ways to Sunday, until she had to get home to her husband and baby.

On her way out, she left me money on the dresser. A guy does that to a girl, and he's a shit, but that was coolest I'd felt in a long time.

And now, she is downstairs in the lobby. They call it a crossroads. I am two months into a four-month treatment program, and I have a big decision to make, something I have historically not done well.

The definition of insanity, right?

Sure, I can leave now, and I can get her to give me the money to get high, and I'll get high, and she'll get high, and we'll get a room at the Four Seasons and fuck on nice sheets with high thread counts, and afterward we'll eat an expensive meal with rare roasted beef and fine red wines at some fancy restaurant, and then we'll go back to the room and we'll get high some more and fuck some more, and a pretty girl will love me again, make me feel safe and forget who I am for a while, and when I put it like that, I don't know how I am able to tell the counselor to please ask her to leave.

28.
Gold Stars

Dear Diary,

I remember listening to Cat Stevens or old mixed tapes of the Pogues and Gene Pitney, and I could feel something then. The music meant something to me, and we'd be sitting there, in somebody's room at Belvedere, having those all-night mad conversations about girls and music, and we were all so young. I never thought I'd have to deal with these consequences.

I'm looking at the cars pass by tonight, high up in this hospital. There is something so lonely about car headlights at night when you watch them from the 9th floor of a mental ward. That's what this place is. Don't kid yourself. It's an insane asylum, a loony bin, a fucking funny farm. Doug E. Fresh would feel right at home.

I light another cigarette, rest my head against the glass, and watch a world below that somehow goes on without me.

"It's so fucked up."

"What is?" Dr. Stevens asks.

"Everything. This place. I mean, they're always telling us in here how smart addicts are, which is bullshit. Have you looked around this floor? Addicts are some of the dumbest people going."

It has been a rough morning. The stars were awarded again, and still no gold one for me, although I think I have been doing a damned good job. I have been moved up to Level II, which means I can leave the grounds for meetings. I participate in all my groups, I tell funny stories, people like me best. Still no gold star. I am pretty sure it's because I've been flirting with the cute blonde who came in last week.

Dr. Stevens seems to genuinely care about me, as though he's taken a special interest in my case. I feel bad that I'm probably going to let him down. I let everyone down. I was talking to one of the counselors the other day, and he told me how a couple years ago, a patient of Dr. Stevens committed suicide. He took it so hard, he had to take a leave of absence. I can't imagine why anyone would enter into this field, nothing but heartache.

Dr. Stevens makes a show of cocking his head and squinting one eye, like he's sizing me up.

"What?" I say. "You know what I mean. It's not just here; it's everywhere."

"What's everywhere?"

"The way it's run. This *place*. This *world*, man. What's the point? To get some shitty job that sucks all your time, jacked up on interest rates and mortgage payments and credit card bills so you can't even afford to see a doctor when you get sick? Busting your ass for a house you never really own, paying rent to a fucking bank, waiting for the wife to split when the money's gone or for the kids to grow up to tell you how much they hate you? And that's *if* you're one of the lucky ones. Where's the payoff? Golf games on the weekend? Disneyland once a year? Until your heart stops beating one day when you're taking a shit and seven people show up to your funeral. This is what they're offering? This is what I'm supposed to get sober for?"

Dr. Stevens starts shaking his head, grand sweeping shakes, big dramatic shakes. "*What* are you talking about? Who are 'they'?"

I take a deep breath and turn away. I don't know what I'm talking about. It's the same lame spiel I've been barking for years, almost on cue and with little forethought, like autopilot ranting. It is the voice of Brian Fast, which burrowed its malcontent into my brain a long time ago and took root, and it's still there, a parasitic worm squirming from the light, searching for new hiding spots to stay alive. And here, it sounds even worse than it did on the streets.

Dr. Stevens rubs his hand over his face, gathers himself to try again. I don't envy his having to work with me.

"What are you so afraid of?" he finally says.

"Christ, don't start with that. I'm not afraid of *trying* or *failing*. Every time I come into one of these places, someone starts with that." I make sure to slow down and enunciate; I have a tendency to talk fast and mash my words together when I get worked up. "It comes down to enjoyment. I don't get enjoyment the same way other people do."

"How do you think other people get enjoyment?"

"Fuck if I know. Their job? Family? Football games? Fucking stamp collecting?"

"When was the last time you had a job?"

I return a blank stare.

"I mean, when you weren't strung out."

"It's been a while—but I know I hated it."

"What were you doing?"

"I worked in a print shop—and I hated it. Get that feeling in the pit of my stomach every morning driving on the 101. That was half my problem, having to show up at that goddamn job every day—have to ask to take a piss, ask to use the telephone, take a day off. A grown man asking to take a piss."

"I'm sure you've lived through worse," he says. "Besides, nobody says you have to go back into that same line of work. Do something you like to do."

"That's the problem: there's *nothing* I like."

"How do you know? When was your last sustained period of sobriety?"

"Define 'sustained.'"

The doctor stands up from his desk, walks behind his chair. I look past him, out the window, at the trees budding, the small pink and yellow flowers pushing through. It's a gray day, but you can tell it is getting warmer outside. I want to be out there.

"Let's try a different angle," Dr. Stevens says. "Why did you come in here? Forget here. Why have you checked in, like clockwork, for the past few years? California. Vermont. Massachusetts. Connecticut. It hasn't been court ordered. You haven't been mandated. In fact, you could leave right now. But you'd be back."

"I run out of money."

Now he returns a blank expression.

I blow out some air. "Because, I mean, it sucks being a junkie; you know that. When I'm running, I look like shit; I hate myself for what I'm doing. I hate what I'm doing to my mother. I have nowhere to sleep. Money's gone as soon as I get it. Everyone hates me. I hate myself. I'm tired of not having a place of my own or trying to keep track of whatever girl I'm running with because she's out doing whatever to get her fix on. I'm sick of being a fucking bum."

"You just told me you don't get enjoyment from anything. What makes being an addict any worse? If that's the way you feel, might as well get high once in a while, right?"

I know what he's doing. It's the same circular reasoning that has dictated my actions for as long as I can recall. Trying to solve an illogical problem with logic. This is a problem that cannot be rationalized away.

"It really is this simple," Dr. Stevens says. "If what you are doing isn't working—and I think we can both agree that it's not—why not try something different?"

We both know he is right, and it's getting harder to ignore, each day growing clearer, with more distance being put between me and the drugs, the times and beliefs that are making less and less sense. What am I fighting so hard to hold onto? Almost everyone I know has already begun the mass exodus out of the city. Do I really want to be an old junkie?

"Listen," the doctor says with a grin, "I appreciate noble causes as much as the next guy. But I don't hear private property owners bitching too much about the evils of capitalism." He looks me in the eye. I try to look away but can't. He moves to the front of the desk, speaks softer. "Let's be honest. Most of these guys aren't going to make it. I'm not saying I ever give up on anybody, but most of them will be back. That's what we do here; I don't kid myself. But I think you have more to offer this world than being another ward of the state." He walks to the door. "You might not believe me now, but trust me, it gets better."

I want to say that it can't get much worse, but I know it can.

29.
Group Part II

Dear Diary,

My mother came to visit me Sunday. That's visiting day here. We went for lunch at her favorite Chinese restaurant. We used to go there a lot when I was a kid. She kept saying how proud of me she is. I tried to temper her enthusiasm. I gave her the discouraging stats and lousy recidivism rate, explained how tough a road this will be, best intentions and all. She wouldn't have any of it. She said I have more will power than anyone she's ever met. I told her this isn't about will power. She said maybe not for most people.

When my mother reached for her water, I could see just how bad her hands have gotten. The scleroderma has turned them into gnarled lobster claws; she pinches at things to pick them up. I want to do this for her. They say you can't do this for another person. But there are only so many times you can break your mother's heart.

She said she is worried about my brother and wants me to talk to him. I reminded her that I only have four months clean; I am not in a position to talk to anybody about anything. Half the days I wake up, find the nearest thing rooted to the earth and hold on for dear life. She doesn't want him to end up like me. I told her that he won't, that he has so much more going for him than I ever did. I said that he sees how bad my life got and won't make the same mistakes. I think I made her feel better. I was lying, of course. Billy is in too far. To get out, he'll have to go through that same machine I did. And it's going to tear him up. As much as I love him, he's on his own. That may sound cold, but if I am going to stay sober, I can't be around him.

As we stood to leave, my mother fell. The scleroderma has started hitting her organs and her circulation is bad. I tried to catch her but couldn't get there in time.

All this shit is so heavy. It's like being back on the Greyhound bus. There are no more funny stories about Rent-a-Center televisions or Spanish markets. Maybe they never were funny. I see why the windows up here are reinforced; some of these stories make you want to jump.

Everything is going fine until we get to the new woman. We can call her June. She looks like a mom, comfortable stretch slacks and durable hairdo, but extra fussy like she's from Greenwich and hasn't farted her whole life. I'd made up my mind as soon as she sat down I didn't like her. It's all too particular, her presentation, like it's been rehearsed, and I don't have sympathy for bored, rich housewives popping pills.

Counselors always ask new arrivals what got them started. It's always the same story, or variations of it, outcasts sneaking Dad's beer, stealing Mom's cigarettes, pot in high school, experimentation leads to bad habits, and on to bigger and worse things. One is too much, a thousand isn't enough, etcetera. June's story is a little different.

June says her troubles began when she was five. She lived in a quiet suburban neighborhood with her mother, who'd had her when she was quite young. There was no father in the picture. Her mother still dated, though, and she didn't want guys to know she had a daughter, so she dug a hole in the backyard, put a door on it. She would lock June inside with a bucket for a toilet. Sometimes her mother wouldn't come home for days. Once she went to Jamaica for a week. The rest of June's childhood wasn't much better, filled with the usual sexual abuse and violence and promiscuity, but it's that story of being buried in the backyard that gets to me. What the hell am I complaining about?

I'm still creeped out following lunch when afternoon session starts and we meet another new patient. We can call this one Ashley. A lot of girls seem to be named that these days. Ashley is young. I don't know how young exactly. You have to be at least eighteen to get on the ninth floor, but she doesn't look much older than that.

Ashley has white-blonde hair, is ridiculously attractive, and flaunts her sex shamelessly, with a tight, little body and big girl curves that let her get away with anything she wants. Black bra straps fall off shoulders, low-rise jeans reveal a thong, bottom lip bit at all the right times. The men act uncomfortably around her, and the women hate her. I wonder why she's not cheering for the home team and having slumber party pillow fights.

When it's her turn to share, Ashley recounts having sex with three men at the same time in the backseat of a car for half a bag of dope. I used to shoot five of those bags at once. She shows little emotion as she's telling this, like she's recalling this one time she ordered a different type of smelly cheese at the market. Ashley isn't sharing this story for shock value or for bragging rights. You learn to read people in places like this. She tells us this story to let us know that nothing is precious to her, that she will always win the battle of who cares less.

Later that night, I walk into the TV room, and Ashley is the only one in there. She lies on her stomach, elbows up, head cradled in hands, watching a program about glamorous women dancing in ball gowns. She peeks over her shoulder, come hither slathered in mascara.

I wince a smile and turn to leave.

"Hey," she says, and I stop. "We should get out of here."

"You haven't been here long enough to get a pass," I say.

Ashley pushes herself up, spins around and leans forward. She isn't wearing a bra. Her nipples are hard. "No, I mean, *get out* of here. Go get a hotel room."

"I have a wife." It's all I can think to say.

Ashley laughs a peculiar little laugh. "What do I care if you have a wife?"

She is gone the next day.

I dial Cathy's number in L.A., but it has been disconnected. I don't want to call her parents' house, but I do anyway and am thankful when no one answers. I leave an extra-polite message.

When we get back from an NA meeting the following night, there's a note on my door that my wife Catherine called. I phone her back, and as soon as she picks up, it's clear something is wrong.

"I'm so glad you called," Cathy says.

"Where are you?" I ask.

"We don't have time for that. Listen to me. They're coming for you."

"Who?"

"The Freemasons." I hear her hand cupped over the receiver. "They're stealing souls again, putting them in the ocean with the brains. *For sale*."

I go somewhere far away as my wife talks about the battered screenwriting guide she picked up in a used book store, how it turned out to have been written by the devil himself, about the car doors slamming with mathematical precision that signifies Armageddon, about the spies who leer in her windows all through the night, about all the single shoes she keeps finding in the street. She says she is tired of voice alterations, "the pointless phone tapping and electronic vocoders muffling incoming messages for anonymity's sake"—when she *already knows* who's calling from the caller ID. She tells me to be careful, that she'd die if anything ever happened to me, how I'm the only one she can talk to or who understands her.

I tell her that is nice to hear.

She wants me to promise I won't let them take my soul.

I tell her I have to go to group and that I love her very much.

She says she will not get off the phone until I promise her I will be careful.

I promise her I will be careful and say goodbye.

30.
Too Old to Die Young

Dear Diary,

I didn't spend most of my days in San Francisco high or sick. I didn't spend them playing music or in jail. I spent them walking and searching the ground. I'd walk from Chinatown to Haight Street and back to the Tenderloin, all the while scanning the pavement. I'd sit at Martin de Porres soup kitchen and eat barley pies and stare at the floor. Yeah, I'd be hoping to find a stray cigarette butt or for money to magically appear, but it was more than that. If you've ever been a junkie, you know what I mean. You get used to being a second-class citizen and keeping your head down. But that wasn't it, either.

I'd walk along the side of the road and rubberneck every passing car. Toward the end, I didn't even know anybody who owned a car, so I couldn't have been waiting to be picked up. It didn't stop me from looking, though, like this ride would get beamed down from the stars with a chest full of answers and a one-way ticket out.

I don't mean for this to sound so morose. I was thinking of the end of Drugstore Cowboy the other day, how after Bob finally cleans up, he tells his ex-girlfriend, "You know, the straight life, for all its trappings, it ain't so bad." And it's not. I'm finding pleasure in the weirdest things these days—a cup of coffee at the Jamaican café by the library, doing my assignments for group, sharing at a meeting, watching

*a towheaded kid hold his mom's hand in a park, baseball
games. I watched a whole baseball game the other night
with Daryll in the TV lounge. I didn't recognize any of the
players, but it didn't matter. We ordered a pizza and watched
the game and we talked about music and writers and, of
course, girls and we laughed at each other's dumb jokes,
and I think I might've been happy.*

They give you two choices in the Advanced program:
get a job or go to school. I'm not sure I'm ready for a job
just yet, but I had a bunch of credits when I went to college
back in the late '80s. I didn't do so well then. I mostly took
classes based on which pretty girl would be where.

There was a flyer on the community bulletin board
about an outreach at my old college, which is just down
the road in New Britain and helps people like me get re-
enrolled. I called the number. Turns out this is the last year
those credits are still good.

I must attend a lot of meetings at the college with
advisors and the woman who oversees the BRS program,
which stands for Bureau of Rehabilitation Services; it is
run conjointly with the State of Connecticut. My mother
is happy to pick me up and bring me to these meetings.
I tell her I can take the bus and that she doesn't need to
be doing this for me, especially with how sick she is. My
mother says doing this for me is the best thing in her life.

The campus isn't like I remember it, even though it
looks the same, for the most part. There are a couple new
buildings and parking garages, freshly paved roads in
and out, but the major landmarks remain: the long, white
administration building with the massive Doric columns,
the giant clock tower, the wide-open grassy spaces, the
ball fields and knolls. I guess I am different.

The woman who works with me is named Noreen. The
BRS program seems designed for people with disabilities,

like students with severe mental or emotional handicaps. When I point this out, Noreen says, technically, that is what I have.

Afterward, I wait to get picked up. Summer's finally here, everything green and muggy in that uniquely New England way. How sweet new-mown grass smells, the air thick with pollen haze and humidity; it's hard to even breathe. My mother doesn't get out of work for another half hour, and it would take me that long to get to Hartford by bus anyway. And I do like to see her smile, even if it's mostly with her eyes these days. The scleroderma has drawn the skin around her mouth so tight, she looks like a cadaver. She's been harping on me for years to go back to school.

I lie on a little hill in the middle of campus under a big oak tree. It is summer session, so there are not many students. But there are some. They walk in little groups, purses and backpacks, ball caps and sneakers, excited by whatever lies ahead. They are all so young.

I drop my head in the grass. The sky swirls vanilla and blue. I watch birds and airplanes and vapor trails. I smell maple and ragweed. Little pieces of cut grass stick to my skin, and I can taste the heat on my tongue. The clock tower chimes.

This seems so far from Hepatitis Heights, the police raids and wretchedness, the skid row rooms and needle exchanges, the dirty clothes and impetigo, the near misses and overdoses, the hunger, the scams and scabies and suicides. If I close my eyes, I can almost believe that was somebody else's life. I'm just not sure that I want to.

Dr. Stevens and I are walking in the pavilion outside the hospital. There's a little rock garden with a miniature waterfall and Japanese bonsai trees, some picnic tables and benches. Often, doctors and counselors eat their meals here. We are the only ones here now. It is hazy, hot and humid, the sun swallowed by thick clouds as an afternoon thunderstorm rolls in. August in New England.

"Sleeping well?" Dr. Stevens asks me. He is dressed in khakis and a bright yellow tropical shirt. I didn't know doctors got "casual Fridays."

"New cocktail's working wonders," I say. "Sleep through the night like a big boy." It has taken almost half a year and a lot of different drug combinations to get me to sleep through the night.

Dr. Stevens holds up his hand for a high-five. I comply, but he can tell by my face that I don't see what the big deal is.

"You don't think that's good?" he asks.

"Sure. I guess. I mean, it's just sleep."

"You know what we've got to do?" He doesn't wait for an answer. "We've got to get you seeing things in a more positive light."

"That's what they've been telling me."

We sit down on top of a picnic table.

I pull my cigarettes from my shirt pocket. "All right if I smoke?"

"I wouldn't recommend it."

"Funny guy." I strike a match.

You can smell the rain through the blanket of heat as you wait for the thunderstorm to erupt. Can feel it in the air, the undercurrent of electricity tickling your skin. I lived through enough New England summers to know when one's coming. I always liked them, the way the cooled winds would swirl just before the cloudburst, exposing the lighter undersides of leaves.

"When do classes start?" Dr. Stevens asks.

There's a playground across the street from the hospital. I watch kids sliding, climbing on the monkey bars, swinging, being kids. It's nice. An ice cream truck bell dings in the distance.

"Two weeks," I say, taking a drag.

"You excited?"

"I guess."

"What do you mean *you guess*?"

"I'm a little nervous. Haven't been in school for a long time. What if I flunk out?"

Dr. Stevens raises his eyebrows, mocking me.

He knows how excited I am. I like having a direction. I'm too old for rock 'n' roll, anyway.

"How long has it been now?" he asks. He means since I last shot heroin.

"Five months, sixteen days, and fourteen hours."

"Not the minutes?" he asks.

"I figured that'd be a bit obsessive."

We don't say anything for a while. I smoke and watch the kids, all different shapes and colors, jumping off swing sets, tumbling in the sand, chasing each other, squealing. I feel a fat raindrop on my hand as the kids scatter for cover. I finish my cigarette, step down and squash it with my heel.

"I guess it's time you get out of here, anyway," Dr. Stevens says. "They're running out of gold stars."

"Funny guy."

"You know, when you first came in, I wasn't sure you'd make it through the night."

I wait. "Neither was I."

31.
A Jog Around the Track

Dear Diary,

I leave today. My mother is picking me up this afternoon. I've been in the hospital for six months. I feel like I should have something amazing to say here, some poignant observation that can make these last ten years mean something, y'know, wrap it all up, like the end of a book or movie. Maybe I can have the hero save the girl one more time, give him another bad guy to defeat. Maybe that's not the point.

I spent ten years looking for cohesion, some unifying principle. I spent ten years looking for answers. And you know what I found? The big secret that I uncovered? Life is unfair.

I go jogging with Daryll. There's a high school with a track five blocks from the hospital. No one seems to mind if we use it. Shortly after we were moved up to Level III, we became eligible to get passes, which means we can leave the grounds unsupervised. We've gone running practically every morning since. Having been trapped inside my head and physically inactive for so long, it feels good just to run and not think.

Watching Daryll jog has been pretty funny. His Hep C is so advanced, his liver suspends over his beltline, bouncing like a stiff, over-inflated beach ball. He can make it around the track once before he gives up and starts walking. I have gotten up to five miles.

Heading back to the hospital, I light a cigarette.

"Got one of those for me?" Daryll asks. Daryll never has his own cigarettes.

The trees tower over us, lush and colorful, pink dogwoods and cherry blossoms, creamy white petals and red sugar maples, intertwined branches and leaves, crisscrossed and crosshatched, trying to block out the sun, but the light still glimmers through. Even in this rundown section of North Hartford, it's beautiful.

We go jogging early in the morning, so hardly anybody is out, everything still and new. An old woman collects her morning paper from the dewy grass. A garbage truck growls in the distance. A cat scales a fence.

We are sweating and smoking, our tendons and ligaments stretched. I feel like I could run another five.

"I'm going to miss you," Daryll says.

"I'll miss you, too. But I'm never coming back to this place."

"That's what they all say." Daryll takes a hard hit off his cigarette, holding the smoke like it's a joint.

We walk up the hill, slowly, toward the hospital.

"What you signed up for?"

"English. Literature courses, mostly." I've been reading incessantly since I got here. At one point, I read fifty novels in fifty days. And that includes the ten it took for *War and Peace*.

Daryll nods approvingly. He's the one who turned me onto Richard Brautigan and *Trout Fishing in America*. We both dig Bukowski and Jim Thompson, pulp noir. Daryll has been trying to write his autobiography in his spare time. He read some to me the other night after AA. It rambles incoherently.

Last week, when we went to the library, Daryll pulled up old newspaper articles on the Internet of all the banks he robbed. Like a footballer whose glory days have passed him by, he beamed, pointing out the parts where neighbors said they were totally shocked because he had "always seemed like such a nice guy."

At the top of the hill, we go through the hospital's employee parking lot, moving past Blue Hills Avenue and toward the hospital entrance.

"Fucking brick buildings," Daryll says, motioning up at the ninth floor. "Why is it I can keep my shit together as long as I have someone mapping out my day for me? But as soon as I have to decide when to eat lunch on my own, everything turns to shit?"

I don't have an answer.

"Let's try and stay in touch, OK?"

I say OK, but we both know we won't. You make friends in these places, as you divulge your secrets and fears. You see each other at your worst. It is such an emotional ride coming off the junk, everything clearing into focus, blues getting bluer, greens greener, all these feelings you've been burying for so long springing back up, helter-skelter and beyond your control, and you're crying at Chunky Soup commercials and cheesy sitcoms, and here are other folks going through the same thing as you. You spend all day in groups and at meetings, talking over chicken pot pies about why your father hated you or about not having a date for prom, the reasons you picked up in the first place. You form intense relationships with these people, propping one another up through a really rough time. Then you never see them again.

"You're too pretty to live like this," Daryll says.

"Stop it. You're making me blush."

As we walk through the hospital's automatic front doors, our shirts heavy with sweat, muscles tender, a cold rush from the air conditioning hits us. Daryll keeps walking to the elevators, but I stop and stand still. I let the cool air wash over me, feeling the little hairs on the back of my neck.

PART FIVE

Epilogue

32.
The Last Round

The doctors couldn't say what finally got her in the end. Everything sort of took over at once. The scleroderma had eaten through her fingers and toes, boring like acid to the bone, connective tissues calcifying, turning her hands and forelimbs to stone, before finally seizing her organs and shutting down her heart. The cancer seemed to sprout inside her all at once, bulbs budding after a hard rain, breasts, lungs, and just about every place else, until there was nothing left to extract or cut out. I was with her at the hospital when she died. I sat there for two days in late January, freezing rain and sleet pelting the window, the dim parking lot lamps unable to light a dreary winter's night as I tried to sum up a life and find new ways to apologize, while my mother lay unconscious, gasping for air like a marooned goldfish.

In those final years, I'd tried to make it up to my mom. Which was pointless. I mean, really, how do you start to make up for that kind of damage?

I was finishing my undergraduate degree at Central Connecticut State University, the first person in my family to graduate college, and had begun applying to grad schools. I'd written a poem about Cathy and Amy, "Saturday Night in the Waning Days of San Francisco," which detailed that last seven-month run. It was a sonnet. I won an award and had it published in the *Connecticut Review.* Afterward, I toured the state with other student writers, getting paid almost $500 to read poetry. A writing professor joked I should enjoy it, since it might be the most money I would ever earn from creative writing.

I was treating school like a full-time job. I edited the university's literary magazine. I worked as a tutor in its writing center. It felt a little weird, being so much older than the other students, but I didn't care; it was helping keep me straight. I once heard that you don't get rid of habits, only substitute them. School was my new junk. I clung to those third-floor English Department offices like a drowning rat.

The wake was held in my small hometown in Connecticut, and it seemed like practically the whole town showed up, despite the freezing temperatures.

It was nice seeing how many people cared about my mother. I'd grown up with these people, gone to school with them, church with them, played ball with them. I never liked most of them, never appreciated any of these small town ties. I could see now they were decent people.

Even though I'd spent the better part of the last ten years in San Francisco, everyone knew about my problems, and any time I came back east, I was sure to champion my screwing up, slinking into local delis and video stores with amped-up sneer and contempt, like my junkiedom were a badge, and as if by doing so, I was exploiting their cowardice for never having left this place, because marrying one's high school sweetheart and working as an insurance broker had to be a failure of imagination. Like so many other things, I now saw I was wrong about that, too.

It was open casket. They'd fitted my mother in a sparking silver evening gown with sequins, the sort of thing she wouldn't want to be caught dead in. It was hard looking at her like that.

Of course you know that the lifeless thing lying there is no longer your mother; it's just a stuffed wax dummy, a representation made-up and cold, put on display so everyone can pay his or her last respects. It's a rite of passage. You get that. But it's also the last time you're going to see any version of her, so you try to will some great emotion, garner some finality in the moment, make it mean more than it possibly can, and when you can't summon these things, you feel like you've let her down all over again.

I wished I could feel something that day, but I couldn't feel much of anything.

People came up to me afterward to tell me how proud my mother had been of me, how all she wanted to talk about over those last few years was how I'd turned my life around. Which I guess I had. But it was still tough to listen to. The biggest accomplishment of my thirty-four years was having climbed out of a hole I'd dug for myself in the first place. Being ignored, even reviled, that I could take, but any time somebody said something nice to me, it stung like hitting an artery.

Big clumps of dirty snow lined Route 71, and it was very cold, not unlike that day in Albany when I climbed the building to jump. The sun dipped low in the winter sky, only a few clipped moments of daylight left. Dump trucks growled up the hill. There was a boarded-up factory across the way, an old paper mill with white washed windows and tire tread scraps, splintered pallets and rusted oil drums. I'd worked there one summer when I was younger. Late-afternoon shadows crept over brown bricks and up the cracked pavement.

Across the parking lot, I saw my brother, Billy, sitting on the bumper of his truck. He'd sat in the front row with me during the service, but we hadn't exchanged more than a few words all afternoon. What was there to say?

Like the city mouse and the country mouse, there is a difference between the city junkie and the country junkie.

The nights I slept under a bridge, the impetigo that scarred my face with rosacea, the daily degradation of slumming for scraps, no one had to see that stuff. They might receive a middle-of-the-night phone call begging for Western Union or help bailing me out of jail, but afterwards they could hang up the phone and be done with me. If you're a country junkie, they see you every day. Your sins are on public display, and it wears on you.

Billy was still working, if sporadically and for several different outfits. Somehow people still trusted him with dynamite, which is a scary thought. My brother's a big man, six-feet-five-inches and more than three hundred pounds, with a voice like he's been up all night chewing on glass. He's four years younger than I am, but he looked ten years older, his once-thick blond hair already thinning, turning grey, deep lines gouging the eyes. His teeth were badly chipped, and he hadn't bothered to fix them. Working in construction, he always smelled like oil and diesel, like our father, and his fingernails were never clean.

I crossed the lot and joined him on the bumper, firing up two cigarettes and passing along one.

I didn't know for sure what drugs he was or wasn't doing. I mean, it's not like we talked about it the few times I'd see him.

When he brought his cigarette to his lips, I noticed the scab on his wrist where he used to fix. It looked fresh.

"You remember that cop in the Caymans?" he said.

Yeah, I remembered that cop in the Caymans. It was after Cathy was shipped to the sanitarium in Minnesota. We'd scored some crack at the Texaco up the street from a dealer named Breeze, when my brother, drunk off his ass on rum, decided to see how fast he could go down the one-lane island road. He had just finished saying, "Look! I'm going a 100 miles per hour!" when we saw the lights in the rearview.

"You're lucky they didn't check your socks," he added with a snicker.

My brother kept smoking, staring toward the ball field where he used to star back in high school. He'd been given a full scholarship to play for Boston College but quit after only a few weeks. I think he was homesick.

"What made you think of that?" I asked.

"I'm thinking of heading down there again. I had it good down there. I liked it there. Maybe I can get my old job back." He waited. "You come and visit me?"

"Yeah," I said, "I'll come visit you."

Guests began filing out of the funeral home, a few looking our way, giving sheepish waves or a nod, dressed in their Sunday suits and long pleated skirts, some ex-classmates with kids of their own now.

As night began to fall, my brother and I talked. About the times he visited me in San Francisco, and the crazy characters like Gluehead and Sanger and Brian Fast, and how we'd stay up for so many days we'd start seeing little glowing electric bugs everywhere. We talked about that time he found me hitchhiking after I skipped out of a rehab up the road, and about that one summer I sent him so much speed he lost close to seventy-five pounds but his head stayed really big, like one of those ballplayers who quits doing steroids. And we talked about growing up together, about our dad and the violence that was never far from us. We talked about our mom. But not about what it would be like without having her around or how much we'd miss her. Instead, we talked about all the fucked-up shit we'd done over the years, like teenagers trying to one up one another, the things we stole from her and pawned and would never get back. We talked about how after she got really sick, we would catch each other stealing her Oxycontins, acting indignant over how anyone could do such a thing to his own mother. And we laughed at all these things, even though we knew they weren't funny.

When we'd finished our cigarettes, I said I should probably go represent the family. Billy said he had to pick up money from a job site, something about needing forty dollars for fuel the next day.

My brother climbed into his truck and fired her up. Its big engine rumbled. He slammed it in gear and lurched over the frozen, plowed mounds of snow and mud, jumping the curb, and trudging up the long, steep hill of Route 71.

I watched him go. His old truck lumbered, rattled, and I wasn't sure he'd make it. Then he reached its crest, and his taillights disappeared out of sight.

I looked down the valley of this place I am from, beyond the mountain where I camped with friends as a kid, and across the turnpike to the edge of town, where tonight high school boys would ride up and down the strip with no particular place to go, hoping to cross paths with the carloads of girls and maybe have something clever to say at a light, but probably not, and so they'd end up like we always did, back on the narrow main drag that leads through the center of town and beneath the trestles that take the trains somewhere else, past the bar and the fire station and the underpass that would soon flood, because it always floods in the spring, where they'd end up sitting on the hoods of cars in the parking lot of McDonald's or in the backs of trucks at 7-Eleven, sneaking tall boys from tailgates no matter how cold it got, until one of the cops drove by and said that it's time to go.

We had a big house back when I was in high school, a two-story, grey Saltbox deep in the cuts on the banks of a pond, only a handful of neighbors for miles. Some nights, when it's very late, I drive there, down twisting roads, even though it no longer belongs to us. No streetlights, country skies black, save for the sliver of moon and little white stars.

Through the woods, I'll come to a clearing where our house still stands, moonlight shining off the water, windows dark. I see the front porch slick with dew, where we always kept a spare key under the milk can. I want to believe that key will still be there, and that when I open the door, it'll be warm inside, and everything will be as I remember it. I'll find my mother and brother asleep, and my old room waiting for me.

I want to be there again, wherever that is now, whatever I have become, because it always feels good to be back home.

ABOUT THE AUTHOR

Photo: Niki Pretti

Joe Clifford is an editor at Gutter Books and producer of Lip Service West, a "gritty, real, raw" reading series in Oakland, CA.

He is the author of the short story collection *Choice Cuts* and the novel *Wake the Undertaker* (Snubnose Press). Excerpts of *Junkie Love* have previously appeared in *Big Bridge*, *Underground Voices*, *Word Riot*, *Fringe*, *Kerouac's Dog's Magazine*, and *POV Magazine*. Much of Joe's writing can be found at www.joeclifford.com.

19907823R00131

Made in the USA
Middletown, DE
08 May 2015